PEACEMAKER
OF
THE PECOS

PEACEMAKER
OF
THE PECOS

C. E. Edmonson

aventine press

Published by Aventine Press
55 East Emerson St.
Chula Vista CA, 91911

ISBN: 1-59330-492-7

Library of Congress Control Number: 2007934448
Library of Congress Cataloging-in-Publication Data
Peacemaker Of The Pecos

www.ceedmonson.com

Printed in the United States of America

For family, for faith

PEACEMAKER
OF
THE PECOS

Chapter One

The sound was of muffled thunder as the herds shifted position. The great plain was black with them, as far as the eye could see, fading into gray hills of stone and mesquite.

The sun-blasted prairie appeared to undulate with movement; heat waves shimmered; the ground trembled. Occasionally a few animals coughed and kicked, while others raised their massive heads and bellowed, as if staking claim to all of Texas.

On the southern edge of the herd, small dust clouds rose. As the riders approached, they could see cracked brown earth and tufts of scrub brush peeking through the breaks. They reined in their horses and dismounted. Overhead, groups of black vultures, called turkey-buzzards by the plainsmen, circled knowingly.

The men were silent as they removed their .50-caliber Sharps rifles and gun-stakes—thin, five-foot high wooden poles with a Y at the top and a sharp spike at the bottom—from sheaths hanging from the high pommels of their saddles. The stakes were the most rudimentary design, contrived for holding the barrel of a long rifle steady for long periods of time.

The riflemen were ten in number, looking alike, hardened men who had been in the saddle for most of their lives. It would have been difficult for a stranger to tell them apart, even from up close.

They were unshaven, with a week's worth of beard-stubble. They wore long, tan dusters that reached down almost to their tarnished spurs. Boots scuffed and worn, wide-brimmed black hats pulled low over their eyes to shield them from the late August sun, they appeared to be drovers or mule-skinners. Only they were not. They were professionals of a different sort, and they took their pay in gold.

They worked full-time for Sam Granger and had already been paid in full for this job. Now it was time to earn their money.

The men fanned out as an arc of a bow, twenty-five yards apart, and fastened the stakes into the earth. Each went into his saddle bags and took out boxes of ammunition, stacking them on the ground. Resting their rifle barrels in the Y of the stakes, they settled in for a long slaughter. The men on the margins fired several shots into the air to spook the buffalo, driving them off their flanks and rear and pushing them toward their front. Once this was done, they were ready to begin the work.

"The Injuns are going to starve this winter," one of them called out, mockingly. "No buffalo—no clothes, no food. Mebbe no war."

"That's good," another hollered, grinning. "Them red devils should all starve, every last papoose and squaw. Must be ten-thousand head in front of us this minute. We can't kill 'em all, least not today. Ain't got the lead—or the daylight."

Now a third man raised the front and rear latch-sights of his Sharps, aimed at the broad-humped quarry and fired, dropping the first animal with a bullet to the skull. The buffalo close by skittered and then lumbered away from it.

"What we can't kill the Army will," he yelled and fired again, a wraith of smoke jerking up from the barrel of his rifle. "If they ain't too busy chasing the Comanch', that is." He turned and looked around. "I hope there's none near here."

His shot had caught the wooly target in the neck. The huge animal plunged to its knees and then crashed onto its side, but did not die immediately. Legs kicking helplessly and blood streaming from its mouth, the bull grunted and wheezed before falling silent and still.

"They ain't near," the first man called. "We'd of seen signs. They're too busy running from Colonel Gregg's bluecoats."

Another rifleman, firing, wasn't as sure. He shook his head. "I don't know," he said. "Them danged Comanches are ghosts. They sneak up on you and you never see 'em. I heard they caught a supply sergeant not fifty feet from the outpost and chopped him up real bad. Over near the Big Bend it was. Let him live, though, even filled his canteen with water for him. But first they cut out his tongue, sliced off his nose and ears, blinded him, and left him wandering around an *arroyo*. When a scout found him, he was near out of his mind."

All of them began firing now, killing the grand beasts as fast they could load, aim and shoot. The air became filled with the sickly sweet smell of blood mixed with the acrid odor of gunpowder and dust. A few of the riflemen's horses whinnied and stamped the ground. But they did not bolt. Purchased by Sam Granger for his men, they were army mounts, used to the sharp crack of gunfire.

"Don't worry," the first man said. "There's none around here. The boss had the whole area scouted and cleaned out. There ain't a Comanch' within a hundred miles." He quit talking and resumed firing.

The sun had begun to slant westward. The ten of them continued their slaughter of buffalo for a number of hours in their effort to deprive the Comanche Indians of subsistence, until hundreds of animals lay dead and dying on the seared plain and flocks of turkey-buzzards feasted on the carcasses.

But the first shooter had been wrong. There were Comanches in the area all right, one Comanche in particular. Two miles off, high atop a mesa, he stood motionless beside his pinto pony. His shoulder-length hair, burnt gold by the sun, streamed backward in the breeze. Tall and spare, dark-eyed and dark-skinned, with a hawk nose and high cheekbones, he wore knee-length moccasins, buckskin britches and a leather vest with no shirt.

He had a carbine slung on his back and two bandoliers of ammunition crisscrossed over his chest. Around his waist was a belted pistol in a covered holster. The holster flap bore the imprint "U.S." and just beneath the letters was a pair of crossed swords. The Comanche was watching the shooting through a pair of field glasses. He intended to remember the faces of these white men.

After a time he lowered the glasses and reached across the back of his horse for the canteen that also had "U.S." on it and, underneath, the same pair of crossed swords. Wiping sweat from his forehead with the back of his hand, he removed the cap and raised the canteen to his lips and took a long drink. Pouring some water into his hand, he splashed it on his face and neck.

He caressed the withers of his pinto, talking softly while it nuzzled him. He reached into the big leather pouch the horse carried and brought out a clay bowl, which he filled with water. With one hand he held the bowl before the horse's mouth. The horse lapped loudly and thirstily at the water. When the bowl was empty he refilled it twice more. Then, putting the bowl and canteen back in the pouch and hanging the field glasses around his neck, he moved to the edge of the bluff, squatted on his haunches, and resumed studying the affair on the plain.

Beneath him, the prairie yawned with death. He saw smoke from the rifles, heard the bellowing of the buffalo, saw the scavenger birds circling the graveyard, and watched the thinning of the herds by the white riflemen in long coats. The West Texas plain had become a carpet of black carcasses.

When he had seen enough, he stood and turned his back toward the shooters and stretched his chiseled arms skyward, as if embracing the winds of the heavens. He spoke a few words, whispered something, walked to his horse and swung lightly up onto its bare back. Face impassive, he tugged the reins gently and the pinto veered and started off down the boulder-strewn slope. The sound of the gunfire remained with him for a long while.

Chapter Two

That same afternoon, twenty-five miles to the west of where the Comanche watched the buffalo falling, William Hart stood along the split-rail fence that enclosed the corral, brushing the coat of the big, spotted-rumped appaloosa.

He was wearing a wide-brimmed planter's hat pulled low over his forehead. His son, in a straw hat with a piece missing from where the dog had grabbed hold of it, stood beside him, observing, but the freckle-faced boy was impatient and in a hurry to be gone.

Having just returned home after taking Billy for a ride over the open plain down near the river, Will passed the brush methodically across the appaloosa's wet flanks and mane.

The westering sun had thrown a long shadow of the farm's windmill across the corral, and Will matched the pace of his brush to the movement of the blades. The horse's hand-tooled black saddle and bridle lay on the ground near the wooden fence-post, the ornamented tack glistening like silver facets with each pass of sunlight.

An expert horseman, Will Hart loved this animal, named Bedford, more than any other horse he had ever owned or ridden, and he had owned and ridden many. Bedford was spirited, yet gentle. Strong and fast and tireless, he was of magnificent build—a beautiful, disciplined mount. Just now Will was trying to teach nine-year-old Billy about proper care and grooming.

"Never let an animal stand in its own sweat and never bring it to a sudden stop after running hard, if you can help it; trot him, walk him, let his heartbeat slow and body cool down, gradually. The way I just did. See?"

"Yes, Pa," Billy said, looking around and rolling his eyes. "Is that how they did it in Mississippi?"

"It's how you do it anywhere, son."

The Hart's farm, 40 acres in Pecos County, had a welcoming peacefulness about it. Located near the junction of Comanche Springs and Horsehead Crossing, it rested close to the banks of the great Pecos River. Passing the Hart farm, the river flowed southeast for more than two-hundred miles and emptied into the Rio Grande below San Antonio near Acuna, Mexico. Its waters helped irrigate Will Hart's crops—corn and wheat and alfalfa. Will Hart made his living raising a few head of cattle and horses, some chickens, and sold milk and eggs and forage in the prairie town of Enterprise, eight miles off.

This was an enchanted country, a land of vast distances, white sunlight and clear air. Will and his wife, Elizabeth, had been married here in this farmhouse and their son had been born in it. Billy and Beth, Will often thought, were as much a part of West Texas as the deer, antelope, wild turkeys, mustangs and even the occasional buffalo herd that roamed their property; only Will hailed from someplace else—Natchez, Mississippi.

Continuing to brush Bedford and trying to explain the proper care of horses to his bored son, Will soon noticed the twin outlines of his wife and Pilar, the dark-haired woman of his *Segundo*—or second in charge, Manolo—step out onto the covered porch of the house built of logs and adobe, fifty yards away. Beth shaded her eyes with her hand as she called to them.

"Will, Billy, supper! Get Manolo and come in. Grandpa's got to leave soon."

Her father, a Methodist minister, was the town preacher in Enterprise, and he had ridden out in his buckboard today to visit. Will could see his rig up near the house, in the shade. The horse was unyoked and tethered to a post.

"Billy," Will said, "go find Manolo and bring him along."

"Do I have to?" Billy said. "Why can't you? I don't want to eat. And I don't want to hear about horses. I'm tired of horses, even Bedford. I want to go fishing."

Just then a long, gangly, tawny-haired mutt, came bounding up from out of nowhere and leaped at Billy, shoving its paws into the boy's chest and licking his face.

"See, Pa, even Lobo wants to go fishing. Can I?"

"Go find Manolo," Will said, "and get inside to your mother. You can fish later; the Pecos isn't going anywhere. Grandpa's waiting to see you."

"Come on, boy," Billy grumbled and trudged off in the direction of the fields where Manolo had been working, the dog wagging its tail happily and running in an angling gait on ahead of him.

Watching them go, Will thought of his own father, who would've given him a hard crack across the face for saying what Billy had said. Will was never close to his father but found himself thinking more and more about him lately. Maybe it was because of Billy's willfulness, much like his own at that age. If Jackson Hart had been more like Preacher Cullen, Will was thinking, his life would've been very different. Maybe then he would not have done things he was ashamed of and hid from Beth. Jackson Hart had been a brute but the things Will had done were not his father's fault. At least the man Beth married was somebody opposite from the one who came from Natchez.

A moment later, Billy returned with the *Segundo* alongside. "Manolo, *que pasa?*" Will said as they neared.

Will and Manolo had been together going on seven years, and he was more like a brother than a hired hand. Manolo Sanchez, who was thirty-five years old, slender and dark, with a scraggly beard on his chin, was a wizard of a herdsman and a magician at making things grow. Under Pilar's watchful eye, he had helped Beth Hart plant the kitchen garden out back of the house, from which most of today's supper was fashioned. Beth's garden grew some of the tastiest corn, bell peppers, onions and cantaloupe in all of Texas.

"*Nada, hombre*," Manolo said. "Fixing fence, stringing wire. Is Pilar up there, in the house?" he asked cautiously, in perfect English but with a Spanish accent of northern Mexico.

"Certainly, man," Will told him.

Manolo shook his head. "Ayee," he shrugged. "I argued with her all last night and again this morning. That *mujer* has finally beaten me with her bullwhip of a tongue. I admit I was wrong. But, *hombre*, she's stubborn."

Will laughed. "Don't apologize to me," he said. "Tell her." Manolo and Pilar were more in love than any couple he knew, with the possible exception of himself and Beth.

"Have no fear," Will said. "My father-in-law is up there, so she'll have to behave. Until after he leaves. And he's leaving soon." He laughed again. "Tell Beth I'll be along in a minute, I'm going to take Bedford in."

Shaking his head, the *Segundo* and the straw-hatted boy beside him headed for the house.

Will bent down and heaved up his leather and led the appaloosa to the water trough inside the barn. He dropped the saddle over a wooden sawhorse. Stepping out, he stopped short when he saw a lone horseman off in the distance.

Shoulders slumped and head down, the rider was approaching slowly and Will kept watching until he recognized him. Then his face broke into a smile.

He stood with folded arms as the horseman drew rein and dismounted from the reddish-brown bay with the black mane. The man was six-feet, the same measure as Will, but a good ten years older. Also like Will, he was clean-shaven and craggy-faced, but this man had a silver star pinned on his leather vest and a pearl-handled Colt .45 Peacemaker revolver in a holster strapped across his chest. He was wearing a dark brown Stetson with a single dent on top and his shirtsleeves were rolled up to the elbows.

"Hello, my friend," Will said. "Good to see you, Noble." The two shook hands warmly and firmly. "Things under control in Enterprise, Sheriff?"

The man looked at him thoughtfully. "For now," he said, in a low, thick voice, with a Mississippi accent similar to Will's. "We need to talk, old friend."

Will clapped him on the back. "Talk we will." He wondered what Noble meant. "Listen. Talking is always best on a full belly. You're just in time to take supper with us. Preacher's here. We can talk afterward."

"Planned it that way," Noble said. "I'm not dumb. The preacher's daughter is one fine cook."

Will led the brown bay into the barn and Noble followed him. The sheriff took off his gun belt, draped it over the horse's saddle and then the two went up to the house.

The fragrance of Sunday supper greeted them. The room was warm and pretty. Will had built the huge stone fireplace himself. The ceiling and walls were of hewn timbers, and the windows were fashioned with inside shutters of wood. Beth had braided the colorful rugs that dotted the planked floor.

Everyone was already seated at the long wooden home-made table that was laden with an abundance of food: leaf greens with sweet yellow onions and chickpeas, roasted red potatoes, pot roast and gravy, loaves of freshly baked yeast bread, and peach cobbler.

"My, this farm of yours certainly is a land of milk and honey," said the gray-haired preacher, wearing a black vest and white collar. "Everything looks delicious, Elizabeth."

Will chuckled to himself as he noticed Manolo sitting as far away from Pilar as the table permitted.

Everyone knew Sheriff Caulder. He took off his hat and shook hands with the preacher and Manolo, and greeted Beth Hart and Pilar Sanchez with a buss on the cheek. "You're growin' like a Texas weed," he said to Billy, playfully rubbing his mop of sandy hair. When the two seated, everyone bowed their heads and Will offered a grace of thanksgiving.

The seven talked of various things as they ate: comings and goings in town, engagements and breakups, the lack of new items in Madison's general store, Texas weather (hot and dry), the birth of Hart calves, the pending mayoral election, and the upcoming church social celebrating the fiftieth wedding anniversary of the town's doctor, Frank Bransom, and his wife, Emma.

After a while, Noble brought up a subject finally of interest to Billy Hart. Bored by the conversation, the boy was furtively passing chunks of beef to the gobbling dog under the table. He froze when Noble uttered what was to him a magic word.

"Not to alarm you unduly," Noble said, "but has anybody seen or heard of any Comanches near your place?" He looked at Will and then at Beth.

"Why, no!" Beth exclaimed, duly alarmed. She shook back her long black hair. "Why do you ask? Has something happened?"

"Comanches?" Billy Hart said hopefully. "Oh, Sheriff Caulder, I'd love to see some Indians! I've seen a few in town, but they didn't look like *real* Indians—not like the ones in my picture-books. Are there really Comanches around?"

"There are no Comanches around," Will told him.

"And quit stuffing that dog," Beth commanded, worried and harsh now because of the conversation. "You're going to make him sick."

"No, no, Beth, nothing's happened," Noble told her. "It's just I've had reports of Comanche riders in the vicinity. Could be they were fleeing the Army. There's been fighting away west and north, up near Fort Stockton, and they could be running for the hills around *Ciudad Juarez*."

"Do you think," the preacher asked, "there's danger here? Should Will and Elizabeth move into town?" He set his cup down and stared at Noble. "No point taking unnecessary risks."

"There's no danger," Will said, glancing at Noble. "And no Comanches. If there were, I'd know it. I'd see the signs."

"Agreed," the sheriff said. He knew Will Hart. "But, as you folks aren't believin' in firearms, I worry about you, alone here, without a weapon." This was why, out of respect, Noble had left his Colt in the barn.

"There's a weapon available, if I need it," Will said, and his father-in-law frowned. "But I don't plan on using one, except maybe to scare off varmints bothering the stock."

"Guns are worse than any Comanche," the preacher said, shaking his head. "Godless instruments for destruction and ruin."

"I like Comanches," Billy told his grandfather. "I like guns, too. I wish I had some guns. I'd protect Ma and Pa and Lobo and kill all the bad people."

"You see?" the preacher said, with a gesture of resignation. "You see what we create? And how would you know, Billy, if someone is good or evil? Can you see the condition of their souls? Only God can see that."

Billy shrugged, and lowered himself in his chair.

"Unless a man is a peace officer, like Sheriff Caulder," the preacher continued, "no one should be permitted to carry a gun. Why, people are shooting each other in our streets every day, everywhere, for base reasons. Newspapers and dime novels celebrate it. It's sickening, this glorification of violence in a supposedly civilized nation."

Beth Hart nodded vigorously in agreement; she detested firearms. As a girl she'd been accidentally caught in a holdup gone bad, a bank robbery in which her mother had been shot and died three weeks later of infection. Rachel Cullen was dead sixteen years now but the memory of that day still lingered in both father and daughter.

"If I see anything," Manolo said, "I get everybody out of here fast and come for you, Sheriff. Don't worry. I always watch when I'm out riding the farm. My eyes are everywhere. And I ride every day. I will protect them."

"You'd better *hombre*," Pilar said, scowling at him from the other end of the table. "If you know what's good for you. If you value your *piel*—your hide!"

"All the same, Will," Noble said, "be careful. Get out at the first sign of trouble. At least the terrain around here is open; you can see all the approaches."

"I'll be careful," Will said. "Always am."

After dessert, Preacher Cullen excused himself and left, as did Manolo and Pilar who went off to settle their dispute. Noble and Will sat sipping coffee and Noble puffed on a soggy cigar. Billy got out his fishing pole and went down to the river with Lobo trailing behind. Beth retired to another room, giving the two men time to be alone.

They talked for more than an hour, reminisced about people they'd known and places they'd seen, until the late sun crept through the kitchen window.

Will, having skirted the issue long enough, said, "So tell me, Noble. What brought you here today? It's always good to see you. But you didn't come for old times, or tales of Comanches. That was for Beth. What's on your mind?"

Noble glanced toward the other room, then leaned forward close to Will's ear. "The Comanches are true," he said. "There have been sightings near here. But, you're right. That's not why I came."

Will nodded. "I know. I've spotted some in the last month. Watching from horseback, at a far distance, peaceful. I'm not concerned. If they were going to do anything, they already would have. I'm no threat. My farm is small and I have nothing worth stealing beyond a couple of horses. So I ask again: why did you come?"

"I've got trouble," Noble said quietly. "Of the kind you were always the best at solving. My deputies have quit in panic and run off. It's *pistoleros*. A pack of them."

Will winced, as if Noble had said "winged demons." He placed his hand over the sheriff's mouth, looked toward the other room, put his finger to his lips and gestured with his head toward the door.

They left the farmhouse as dusk was falling and walked down to the corral. Will smelled oats mingled with newly turned alfalfa, heard the snorting of the horses in the barn and the chirping of the crickets in the sagebrush. The sun setting behind charcoal clouds had streaked the darkening sky purple; ochre rays tinged with blue tinted the horizon and radiated in all directions like the spokes of a wagon wheel.

"How many *pistoleros*?" Will asked. He leaned against the gate, one boot up behind him on the slat.

"Right now, maybe fifty guns."

Will's face grimaced.

"Already in town, taking every room in Baylor's hotel. With more on the way. They're due in a day or so off the Overland Stage."

"Why?"

Noble grunted. "Sam Granger needs his flunky, Mobley, to win the mayor election."

"I've heard about Granger," Will said.

"He's taking no chances. Knows most folks hate him, and hate Mobley, and hate their railroad friends from up North. Knows folks won't vote for the railroad coming to Enterprise and making a cesspit of it. These *pistoleros* are out of New Mexico Territory, fresh from the Turner-Mansfield cattle war, with blood on their saddles. They call themselves 'Regulators' and go around in long trail coats, the whole bunch. Granger imported them for some friendly persuasion. Figures bullets are surer than ballots."

"Persuasion with Colts," Will said.

"Exactly. They're here for another reason besides," Noble told him.

"What's that?"

"As a private militia, to assist the Army in stopping Comanches from attacking their precious railroad and interfering with the laying of track. Granger is bent on getting the railroad in, so he can ship his longhorns easily to Abilene and St. Louis. And build more saloons and gambling parlors and other such to attract every drover, rustler, pickpocket, gunslinger and saddle tramp from here to Amarillo; and wind up owning half of Texas. He already owns half of New Mexico. And that's just a territory. We're a state, with political clout, now that Reconstruction's over. Granger aims to become a king. Which is fine by me. As long as his men don't break the law. It's my bad luck that they already have."

Will was silent. "Do you know any of these regulators?"

"Can't say. I've only met their trail boss, or foreman, or whatever the heck he is; he dropped by my office this morning. To clue me in he was going to be around with his boys. To try to frighten me."

"And did he?"

"What do you think?"

Will stared at him. "I think you should leave these *pistoleros* alone. Stay out of their way. This boss, has he got a name?"

"Marlowe. Zach Marlowe. Tall as you and me, a soft voice with a Yankee accent. Got a drooping mustache. Totes two Colt pistols with black onyx handles. Ever run across him?"

"Haven't had the pleasure. Heard the name, though. Cole Younger mentioned him to me. A long time ago."

"What did Cole say?"

Will shrugged. "That Marlowe earns top dollar; he's a top gun. Doesn't care how he uses it or who for. Cole didn't like him, called him a back-shooter."

Noble leaned back against the gate with both elbows resting on the wooden brace, close to Will.

"Now you know why I came."

"The answer is no," Will said, looking off toward the setting sun.

But he was concerned. Noble Caulder was one of the bravest, most proficient fighting men he had ever known. If Noble was desperate enough to come here asking an impossible thing, the situation had to be worse than he let on.

The look on Noble's face showed the struggle he was facing. Will knew what his friend must be going through—he had been there. But that was a long time ago.

Noble came off the fence now, turned and faced Will. "Listen, old friend. Forty guns I can handle. But fifty? I'll leave ten for you."

"Ten is an unlucky number for me. You know why. I'll never buckle a gun on again. So my answer has got to be no. Dang it, Noble, just let these regulators do whatever they'll do. The railroad's coming anyway, regardless of what you, or the people of Enterprise, or the Comanche Indians, or anybody else wants. It's called Manifest Destiny, to put it politely, and it doesn't matter to the power-brokers how many innocent people have to die to bring it about. Didn't we see that in Dixie for four bloody years? Don't mix up in something you can't control. Leave Granger and his gunmen alone."

"I can't."

Will hung his head and looked soberly. "I know."

"I'll ask again, Will. Come with me. Together we can solve this problem. I'll have you home the day after the election, in less than a week. That's guaranteed."

"Fifty, a hundred to one? Those are mighty long odds."

"We've beaten long odds before. Together, we can do it again."

"Not interested, Noble. I can't say it plainer. I'd do just about anything for you, but don't ask this. *This I cannot do.*"

"Listen, Mister," Noble said, his voice rising. "You owe me. I saved your bacon at Corinth and again at Brice's Crossing. Have you forgotten? Now I need a favor."

There was an awkward silence as a wall formed between them.

"No, I haven't forgotten," Will said finally, in a low voice. "And I never will. But I owe my wife and son too. I don't care so much about my life, but Billy needs me. Beth is still young but can't have any more children; she was fortunate to conceive Billy; nearly lost him. Even if I wanted to get involved—which I don't—can you imagine what she would say? My marriage would be over. All I want now is to work this little place, love my wife, and raise my boy. I owe you, yes. But I owe you most for the happiness I have. If you hadn't brought me down here, I wouldn't have known Beth. Sure, I owe you. It's a debt I can never repay."

Noble sighed and smiled in the dark. A cool night wind had set in. "You don't owe me," he said.

Will felt the iron clasp of his friend's hand on his shoulder.

"I invited you here to start fresh. Who knows better than me what you've been through, what you've been and what you've done? What happened for you and Beth was fate. It had nothing to do with Noble Caulder. I'm sorry for coming here, Will. Forgive me."

"There's nothing to forgive. But listen: send for the U.S. Marshal. I'll feel better."

"I would, but he couldn't get here before the election anyway, if he'd come at all. Granger's got a ton of pull with his carpetbagger friends."

Noble took out his pocket watch which hung from a chain on his belt. "But now, I see it's time to be getting along; it's late. Say goodbye to Beth for me, and tell her I'm much obliged for that fine supper."

"I will do that." He stepped up close to Noble and the two embraced. "Come on," Will said to him. "I'll walk you to your horse."

Beth was in their room when Will went in, lying on her back beneath a blanket of patchwork and reading by the weak glimmer of a kerosene lamp. He noticed her mass of dark hair spread prettily all across the pillows she had behind her neck. She set the open book down on her lap and looked up as he entered.

"Hello, stranger," she teased, her brown eyes flashing.

"Hi." He removed his hat and set it on the bureau in front of the mirror. "What are you reading?" he asked.

"A book of stories, *Twice-Told Tales*. By Nathaniel Hawthorne. He's a good writer, for a Yankee."

"And you're the most beautiful belle ever," he said.

"Why, thank you, kind sir," she smiled. "Did you have a good visit with Noble?"

"I did."

"I'm glad. I know how you love him."

He went over to the bed and sat beside her on the edge. "Do you know how I love you?"

"No," she said. "I've forgotten. Tell me again. And again. And again."

"I love you more than anything in this world, or in any other, Beth."

Will went down the hall to Billy's room and quietly cracked the door and peered in. He smiled as he saw his son curled tight in a corner, sound asleep, while the dog was sprawled across most of the bed sleeping on its back, all four paws in the air.

He returned to the bedroom and began taking off his shirt. "He's out," he said to Beth.

Will stood at the foot of the bed looking at her. He felt his stomach turn over, the way it always did at moments like this, the way it had for the past ten years. No woman had ever moved him this way, not even Abby, and no one else ever would again or ever have the chance.

As they kissed, Will wondered which was truer in him: what he had done in the last decade as a husband and father, or what he had been in the years before that. He longed to ask Beth the question and hear words of reassurance; but he could not ask it. That was a conversation they would never have. Will hated to keep things from her, above all these things that Noble's visit had made him remember. But there was nothing for it. If he wanted to hold onto her, she could only be permitted to know him this one way.

They lay there, one hand holding the other, looking out the window at the rising moon and starlit sky.

"I think I'll go into town in the morning," he said.

"For what? We don't need anything."

"I know. But I want to stop at Madison's and look at some gear I saw in his farm catalogue. Then I think I'll swing by the church and see if your father needs any help getting ready for the doc's anniversary party. I can take Billy along."

"Good," she said and kissed his nose. "He'll like that."

"Good," he said.

Will closed his eyes, but sleep did not come easily. He found himself wide awake, keenly sensitive to the moan of the wind winnowing through the shutters and the sharp call of coyotes off in the distance.

He did not tell Beth his real reason for wanting to go to town. He was thinking about Noble again. And he was very worried.

Chapter Three

Whirling clouds of red sand jigged across the road leading into Enterprise. The sun was high in the sky and there was heat in the air. Billy wrinkled his freckled nose at the scent of the stockyards on the edge of town.

William Hart steered the wagon up the dusty street and reined up easily alongside the old church. The weather-beaten wood structure with peeling paint had been built by the Society of Friends in 1830, almost fifty years earlier. The original bell tower and a white cross rose from its roof. The church and the town cemetery were situated on the northern edge of Enterprise at a grove of cottonwoods, just beyond the point where the main street came together with a few scattered clapboard homes skirted by whitewashed picket fences.

Will dismounted, and with strong hands helped Billy down from the high seat of the wagon. Tall in stature and straight-shouldered, Will paused for a moment, watching two horsemen in long trail coats slowly make their way down toward the center of town. He wondered if he knew them, but could not tell from that distance.

The day was sunny and a little cooler than it had been in the last few weeks, although still quite warm. Will tethered the four-horse team to a hitching post beside the water trough, and took out his pocket watch. It was half past the noon hour. Billy pumped a couple of gushes of fresh water into the trough, and took off up the dirt path ahead of Will. The dog, Lobo, leaped down from the wagon, bounded after the boy and followed him into the church.

"Stay here and help Grandpa finish decorating while I go down to Madison's," Will called to his son. "The Bransom's anniversary party is tomorrow and we need to be ready."

"Okay, Pa. Aren't you coming in to say hi to Grandpa?"

"I will," Will nodded, and smiled. "But only for a minute."

Wanting to see if trouble was brewing in the streets of Enterprise and what Noble might be doing about it, Will felt uneasy. The sheriff, he knew, would try to arrest the *pistoleros* in town, regardless of their number, if they so much as spit on the sidewalk. But, as he also knew, these men were different than any that had ridden into Enterprise in the last ten years. They were not mere cowboys looking for a good time. And they would not be cowed by the sight of Noble's star and his shotgun. Here, now, were fierce, deadly men, the worst of the worst. To Will Hart they were the blight of the earth.

He found Preacher Cullen in the fellowship hall, where the reception, dancing and eating would take place, standing on a chair and tacking up colored streamers. The preacher was in his shirtsleeves and suspenders and beside his chair was Mrs. Madison, the white-haired wife of the owner of Madison's general store. She was wearing a blue-hooped skirt and matching bonnet, her kind face worn and well-lined. Over her arm hung a cutout of connected, yellow cardboard letters. Will leaned over to read them. They spelled HAPPY ANNIVERSARY.

"Afternoon, Ma'am," Will said, touching the brim of his hat. "And good day to you, Seth," he greeted his father-in-law. "I've brought you a pair of helpers. One's got two legs and the other has four."

"So I see," Preacher Cullen replied with good humor, glancing down at his grandson, running around the hall playing tag with the dog's tail and swiping at it with his straw hat.

Will saw that the tables and chairs were already set up and that there was a place reserved in the corner for the fiddlers and other musicians. Looking up, he read the large cross-stitched sampler, framed prominently in the center of the back wall:

Blessed are the peacemakers,
for they shall be called the children of God. Matthew 5:9

These were fine words, Will thought whenever he saw them. He wondered if there would ever come a time when Americans, Northerners or Southerners, white or black or red or brown, could put them into practice. *Not today*, he worried. *Not in Enterprise.*

"Sir," Will said. "I'm going down to Madison's, unless you need me to do anything."

"No, go on," the preacher mumbled, a tack between his lips. "I've got my helpers and Julianne is here."

Will smiled at Mrs. Madison. "Is your husband in the store?"

"Yes, Will. Lucas is there," she said. "He's got some things put away for Beth."

"Good. Then I'll be going. Billy, mind your grandfather while I'm gone."

"Okay, Pa," Billy said, still chasing the dog.

Will set off on foot for the center of town. Hat pulled low over his forehead so that his face was barely visible, he walked slowly, his head forward, but his keen eyes sweeping from side to side, carefully sizing up the activity in town. The main street was wide and lined with numerous structures—some brick or stone, some timber, but mostly red adobe—fronted by hitching rails and a few saddled horses.

To all appearances, Will was just another citizen out for a stroll in the afternoon sun. But his ever-watchful gaze was different from those of ordinary citizens. They were trained to look for different things.

Passing Granger's livery stable, he noted that it was filled to capacity with horses, along with blankets, weapons, and spare parts for buckboards and saddles and bridles. He slowed his stride as he neared the Overland Stage offices, came to the Wells Fargo building, and then the sheriff's office next to it. Will stopped and looked through the window. Noble was not in. He tried the door; it was bolted. The jail cell was open and Will registered that there was an empty slot in the gun rack behind Noble's desk.

He moved on, crossing to the other side of the street. He tipped his hat to several ladies as he passed Baylor's hotel and the Lone Star bank, greeted several townsmen walking by, smelled fresh-baked pie as he passed by Ma Hanley's cafe, and continued toward Madison's store. Will heard piano music and raucous laughter as he approached Spanish Red's; that was where he first spotted them.

Four armed men in unbuttoned dusters and dark wide-brimmed hats suddenly came out the swinging doors of Spanish Red's, right in front of him. Two of them carried bundles of black-lettered handbills that said ELECT MOBLEY, MOBLEY FOR MAYOR. When Will accidentally bumped into the man in front, the *pistolero* turned and shoved him hard, driving him into the wall and nearly knocking him over onto the boardwalk's wooden planks.

"Watch out, farmer," the regulator growled.

Without a further look at Will, he took out his gun, reached into the pocket of his coat and removed a few nails. He grabbed several posters from his companion and, using the butt of the revolver, tacked them up beside the doors of Spanish Red's.

Will caught his balance and straightened up. Careful to make no gesture that could be viewed as threatening, he watched the movement of their hands. But the four ignored him and headed off. They split up and began abruptly confronting each person they encountered.

Thrusting their handbills into pockets and purses, even into one baby carriage, they harangued the townspeople. "Mobley equals progress and better times," they said, passing out the bills. "Vote for Mobley and the Railroad. Or," they warned, "life in Enterprise will get very ugly."

Everyone understood that the threat came directly from the mouth of Sam Granger.

To underscore it further, when a crippled Confederate veteran protested that the War and Reconstruction were over and that Enterprise was free and self-governing, a regulator stuffed a handbill into his mouth, slapped his face and flung him down into the street.

"You Rebs shouldn't even be allowed to vote," the regulator told the old soldier. "So, you'd best be sure it's for the right people."

Swaggering up main street, spurs jingling, the regulators continued their campaign.

Will leaned against the wall of Spanish Red's and watched them. Some customers poked their heads out and asked what was going on.

"Politics," Will told them. "Granger-style." He turned and went down to Madison's.

Will noticed three rather fine horses with Mexican saddles tied to the hitching rail in front of the store. He stepped closer to the door-post and peered in. On the counter lay open crates of fresh produce and eggs. The long shelves behind the counter held a generous supply of canned goods and household provisions. The floor was lined with stuffed sacks of flour and seed, a few farm implements, and wooden kegs and barrels of various sizes.

Will spied Lucas Madison in his white apron standing near the cash register. His usually good-natured face was furrowed and wearing a terrified expression. He appeared to be hiding behind a pair of coffee-filled glass jars. Two regulators were there, along with Roy Granger, Sam Granger's only son.

On seeing Will, Lucas tossed his head toward the door indicating that he should get out.

Half inside, Will saw straight away what was frightening the storekeeper. An elderly Indian, with gray braids hanging from under a round hat with a feather in its band, was being tormented by Roy Granger.

Twenty-five years old, stoop-shoulder and bowlegged, Roy wore leather chaps and a tied-down gun on his right hip. He had a reputation as a bully and was used to throwing his weight around. He had hold of the Indian by the shirt and was shaking him back and forth.

"This is a store for white folks," Roy said into his face. "We don't allow redskins in here. Didn't you read the sign? *No Injuns allowed.* Savvy, Comanch'?"

"I come to buy present for granddaughter," the disheveled Indian said in apology, wiping sweat from his forehead. "I not see sign."

This was because there was no such sign.

Will stepped inside and slammed the door, rattling the shades. Everybody stared at him. The two men with Roy—gun-belted, dusty-booted, with long coats—had their faces in shadow under wide-brimmed black hats.

Will looked at Lucas Madison and casually walked over toward the register. From the corner of his eye he carefully watched Roy and the two regulators.

"Good afternoon, Lucas," he said. "Julianne tells me you have something for Beth."

Lucas Madison was wide-eyed and swallowed hard, but said nothing.

Roy Granger turned back to the Indian. "Don't give me no Comanche sass," he jeered. He hit him across the face with his open hand, leaving a mark on his sallow cheek. "My father is going to clean out Texas and get rid of all you murderin' savages."

"Seems to me," Will said to Lucas Madison, raising his voice, "that the least folks ought to do is get their hatreds right."

He rested his back on the counter, folded his arms and looked over at Roy. "He's not Comanche," Will said. "He's Mescalero-Apache. From the reservation."

Roy Granger glowered at him. "What, are you some kind of expert on redskins?" He did not like being interrupted. "Tribes don't matter; they're savages. They're all the same."

Will shook his head. "How can that be?" he asked, in a friendly tone. "Just, for example, take Mr. Madison here. He's as white as you are. Maybe whiter. But, he's nothing at all like you." He smiled. "You see? Don't be so quick to judge."

Roy Granger cocked his head and narrowed his shifty eyes at Will, hesitating, uncertain of what he meant. He decided it didn't matter and refocused his attention on the old Apache. Grabbing him by the throat, he threw open the door and dragged him out to the street, where he began beating him with his fists.

Will took out after him to stop it. But he halted in mid-stride when he felt the hard push of cold steel against the back of his neck.

"Don't do it farmer," a gruff voice warned. "Stand and let it happen." The regulator leaned close and muttered in Will's ear. "You've got grit," he said, a short cigar clenched tight between his teeth. "But you're plumb *loco*. Don't you know who that boy is? That's Roy Granger, son of Samuel Granger. Mr. Granger is the most powerful man in these parts and may wind up President. Grangers do whatever they want."

Will glanced sideways. "I'm unarmed, as you can see," he said. Hands at his sides, Will turned and looked at the pair of regulators. The one with the Colt on him was of short stature compared with the other. A sudden smell of bourbon and tobacco wafted off the two.

"You must be proud of these Grangers," Will said. He was on the boardwalk just outside the door of Madison's store with the pistol against his neck. The man with the gun stood beside him.

The man shrugged. "They pay high wages."

"Some things shouldn't be for sale."

Will and the *pistoleros* stood and watched the scene unfold. The old Apache had crumpled to the ground. Roy Granger commenced kicking the Indian with his square-toed boot, but halted when he saw a tall figure approaching up the middle of the street. Recognizing him, Roy made a grab for his pistol but stopped in mid-lunge. He ducked his head, cringing at the sound of a shotgun blast. The trio of horses in front of Will threw up their heads and snorted, but did not bolt or break tether.

The man with the shotgun in the air lowered the barrel and trained it on Roy. He had on a tan Stetson, carried a pearl-handled Colt .45 Peacemaker revolver in a shoulder holster, and wore a silver star on his shirt.

"You again," Noble Caulder said, disgusted, stepping up and pressing the shotgun into Roy's chest. He pushed him back several feet from the Indian kneeling on the ground. "Unbuckle. You're coming in. What do you think you're doing?"

"It's just a danged savage," Roy told him, mockingly.

His eyes and shotgun leveled on Roy, Noble bent down and helped the old Indian to his feet. "Go see the doc and tell him I said to fix you up. Down the street, to the right."

The Apache grunted, dusted himself, picked up his hat and shambled away on unsteady legs.

"You all right, Will?" Noble called up, squinting in the fierce sun.

"I'm all right," Will said, keeping a keen eye on the crowd for any outbreak of regulators who might decide to rise in defense of Sam Granger's son.

"Holster that shootin' iron," Noble told the regulator beside Will. "Unless you want some of this." He swung the shotgun toward him. "No need to move, Roy. Twitch, and I'll break your skull."

Roy cursed under his breath, and with cocky exaggeration, he slowly unbuckled his gun belt and dropped it in the dirt.

The regulator stood hesitating, mouthing his cigar.

"Think, man," Noble said. "Is it worth dying for?"

Finally the gunman lowered his pistol and holstered it.

"All of you, move. You better come along, too, Will."

The five marched up the street with the sheriff trailing, his shotgun held waist-high, cradled in the bend of his arm, and aimed at Roy. A curious crowd began gathering along the plank sidewalks in front of stores to watch their progress; even the owner of Spanish Red's, Jorge Velasquez, came out. Some of his girls came too, bedecked in their dark stockings and gaudy red dresses. With whispers and low breath, the townspeople watched. Everyone feared a storm was brewing in Enterprise.

Noble put Roy and the two regulators inside the jail-cell and locked them in. He motioned Will into one of the chairs near his desk in the outer office.

"Caulder, you no good…," Roy snarled from behind the bars. "My father will have your two-bit tin star for this. Who do you think you are? My father will have us out of here in five minutes, and I wouldn't want to be in your boots when he does."

"Oh, hush up, you spoiled little boy," Noble said. He stood the shotgun back up in the gun rack. "Do you want me to wash your mouth out with lye and send you to bed hungry?" He plunked himself down in his swivel chair, put his feet up on the desk and crossed his legs.

"You'll regret this, old man," Roy yelled. "You're going to be sorry."

Will leaned forward. "This kid is bad news."

Noble rolled his eyes. "You don't know the half of it. What happened down at Madison's?"

Will told him. He also told about the regulators intimidating the voters of Enterprise, of which Noble already knew.

"Will you testify to all that in court?" the sheriff asked.

"Yes."

"Good. Will Lucas Madison?"

"Probably not. He's mighty frightened."

Roy Granger now began ranting again. "You'd best let me out, Caulder. I'm warning you. You can't lock me in here because of some filthy redskin. Now fetch us some coffee and some grub—we've worked up quite an appetite!"

"They won't draw much of a sentence for assault," Noble said to Will, ignoring the prisoner's shouts. "But that doesn't matter. The message will go out. Enterprise belongs to its people. Not to Roy and Sam Granger. And for sure not to any *pistoleros* from up North. I'll take my oath on it."

This was one reason Will admired Noble, forever strong and proud and fearless. But too fearless now, and as stubborn as a rusty hinge, reckless even, alone, with no deputies. Will felt the guilt of having refused to help his friend churning in his chest.

"Watch yourself, Noble. These *pistoleros* look qualified."

"They'll need to be," Noble snorted. Then, "Maybe I'll get lucky and they'll see reason."

"Be careful, old friend."

Just then the office door opened and two men entered. One was a regulator in a long coat; Will had not seen him before. The other, with a dark-haired young woman on his arm, was Sam Granger.

He was hatless and wearing an elegant blue suit that fitted him well. Beneath his cutaway was a silk vest, starched white shirt and white silk cravat. Slim and of medium height, weak-chinned, with a mustached face lined and sunburned, he looked to be about sixty years of age. The woman with him was pretty and carried a fancy parasol; she appeared to be no more than half his age.

"Sheriff Caulder," he said in a deep baritone. "I heard what happened. I'm here to offer my sincere apology and to pay for any damages my foolish son may have inflicted. His bad manners are my fault."

"Daddy? Is that you?" Roy called happily. "You see, you dumb old man," he yelled to Noble. "I told you."

"Shut up, Roy," Sam Granger ordered. "I'll deal with you later."

His accent was Northern, of Massachusetts. Sam Granger hailed from a small town outside of Boston. He had made much of his fortune in currency speculation and railroad stocks after the Panic of 1873. But, greedy, grasping and ambitious, he wanted more. Needing elbow room, he headed south and west to see what he could squeeze from the prostrate former Confederacy.

Endless opportunity beckoned in a region where land and beef were both plentiful and cheap. Settling on the Texas frontier, he learned that was equally true of life itself.

Rumors abounded that Sam Granger had paid to have murdered the husband of the woman now at his side, Magdalena, and forced her to live with him. No one had ever proved anything one way or the other, yet people believed it. As an empire-maker and power-broker, there were legions of desperate men anxious to perform all sorts of despicable services for him, for money.

"It didn't take you long," Noble said.

"Bad news travels fast," Sam Granger replied. "Maggie and I were in town anyway."

"No doubt," Noble said, raising an eyebrow. "Working to rig an election."

"I wouldn't say that. People have a right to campaign and agitate for their political choices."

"You mean *your* choices," Noble said.

"The right choices for Enterprise. In case you haven't heard, I've been buying tracts of land in the Pecos region and working to route the railroad through my properties. The people in this section of the country are stiff-necked and backward-thinking. It's past time they caught up with the nineteenth century. Heck, almost the twentieth. We're a modern nation. Aaron Mobley understands this, and that's why I'm backing him."

Will stood now and faced him. "Do modern times call for starving and exterminating Indians with a private army?"

Granger grew angry but controlled it. He wiped his perspiring face and breathed deeply. "Listen, Sheriff. I don't intend to send my steers along the Chisholm to Abilene any longer. They get lost, sick, rustled, and attacked by redskins. The Army is only too glad of my help. Railroad lines and workers need protecting, and it's a big country. Soldiers can't be everywhere."

"The Indians aren't interested in your beef or your profits," Noble said. "All they want is for treaties to be respected and the buffalo left alone. But the railroad keeps robbing their land. Enterprise doesn't want your railroad either, not with the element you'll bring, an element to make you richer than Croesus. I'd say you have a couple of problems."

Sam Granger smiled thinly. "The folks here are decent, but know little about the outside world. They'll learn to understand the benefits and thank me in due course. The railroad will enrich their lives. As for the Comanche trying to hold back the future, I refuse to permit a handful of savages to block the progress of millions of Americans."

"So you butcher the buffalo?" Will asked. "To bring progress? And, just for the record, Comanches *are* Americans. But they can't eat your progress."

Granger's face reddened. He raised his voice, and pounded a clenched fist on the desk. "If the Indians are hungry, let them choke on *choya* thorns for all I care. Or go further south into Mexico."

The regulator in the background now eased forward and stood staring coldly at Will. He had two black-handled pistols on his hips in turned-around holsters. Will could make out a number of notches filed on the handles.

"Who's *this*, Sheriff?" the regulator inquired to Noble.

"What's that to you, Marlowe?" Noble said bluntly.

Will stared back, studying Zach Marlowe. The thumb and forefinger of both his hands, Will noticed, were heavily calloused. This, he knew, was caused by the repetitive firing of single-action revolvers. Dark-eyed and stubble-faced, the regulator had a drooping mustache and sunken cheeks and wore a soiled yellow scarf around his neck.

"Mr. Marlowe is a close associate," Sam Granger said. "As I own various businesses and can't devote time to all, he has a contract to look after certain of my interests. Tell me, Sheriff Caulder, is this the man who witnessed the ruckus in which an Indian insulted my son and caused him to be arrested?"

"I am," Will said, grinning. "Except that isn't what happened."

"And you are?"

Before Will answered, Noble said quickly, "A concerned citizen."

"Well, Mr. Concerned Citizen," Zach Marlowe said stepping closer to Will. "People need to be real careful about sticking their noses in other men's business. That's how noses get chopped off. But maybe you're not exactly sure what took place. Maybe you didn't see what you thought you saw. Maybe you saw something else. That can happen in heated moments. I guess you couldn't honestly swear to anything in court."

Will took Zack Marlowe's eye and held it. "The kid beat a helpless old man for fun. That's what happened in your 'heated moment.' Just that. You savvy, *pistolero*?"

Noble took his feet off the desk and stood between the two. He did not want Will getting into it with Marlowe. He ignored the regulator and spoke to Sam Granger. "Did I just hear your man threaten a citizen of this town?"

Granger looked hard at him. "No threat; a piece of friendly advice." He turned to Will. "I'd call it a sound judgment."

"All right, Granger," Noble said. He was fast losing patience. "You didn't come here to spread pearls of wisdom. What's on your mind?"

Sam Granger reached into his inner jacket pocket, took out a big leather wallet and peeled off several large bills. He spread them out on Noble's desk. "I'm paying the fine and the bail for these men. I've already seen Judge Fenton. He assessed the amount and said I could pay you. If you don't believe me, ask him yourself."

"Oh, I believe you," Noble said.

Stuart Fenton, Will knew, was not the man to deny Sam Granger anything. Fenton had a fondness for whiskey and cards, but that was not bad. What was bad was that he was for sale and Granger had bought him.

Noble went to the cell. Rattling keys, he unlocked the door and the three emerged.

Roy sauntered out before the other two, stopped in front of Noble and grinned. "Didn't I tell you? I'll see you soon, old man. Real soon."

"You better hope not, boy," Noble said and gave them back their weapons. Looking at Will, he said, "You can go, too."

"Noble, I..." Will started.

"Go home," interrupted his friend. "Give Beth my best. I'll see you all tomorrow evening."

Will walked out into the bright sunlight, and made his way toward the church to get Billy and head home.

The Grangers, the woman, and the three regulators left the office and stood talking outside the open office door. Sheriff Caulder watched them for a moment and was surprised when Sam Granger made a sweeping, backhanded motion with his right arm and struck his son viciously across the side of the face. Roy looked stunned.

"I'm in the middle of something big and you pull a stunt like this?" the elder Granger flashed. "Then, you embarrass me by letting that Sheriff take you in like a common derelict? And two bodyguards watching your back!"

"It's their fault, Daddy," Roy said, red-faced and rubbing his jaw. "They should've taken Caulder. You should fire them, or worse."

"It's *your* fault," Sam roared. "You're a Granger. They're employees, not ownership. They did their job. I expect you to succeed in whatever you do, but you've disappointed me again. Now, get out of my sight. And remember what I said."

The group broke up and left in separate directions. But Roy motioned Zach Marlowe over, and whispered something to him. Marlowe looked at his pocket watch, and nodded. The two headed off singly: Marlowe went up main street, and Roy headed toward Spanish Red's.

Later that afternoon, a few minutes before five o'clock, Roy Granger waited in front of the livery stable. Roy was still fuming over the way Noble Caulder and his father had humiliated him in public. Now he was going to show them that he too carried clout, that he too was a man to be feared and respected. He would do some electioneering of his own. He would make certain the vote went their way by removing the last obstacle to victory.

Zach Marlowe showed up promptly on the hour. Roy issued orders to Marlowe, and the pair walked toward the center of town, boots thumping on the boardwalk.

The two walked about fifty yards, rounded a corner, and stopped in front of the law offices of Collier and Philippe. Peering in through the window, Roy saw both lawyers seated at their desks. He knocked on the door.

"Who is it?" one of the men inside asked.

"Roy Granger. Here to see Isaac Collier."

Isaac Collier was the political opponent of Aaron Mobley in the upcoming mayor's election and was a heavy favorite. Collier was running on the democrat ticket and Mobley the republican.

Collier unlatched the door and opened it. "What do you want?" he said stiffly.

"I just want to talk politics for a minute," Roy said. "I have a message from my father. Can we come in?"

The attorney nodded and motioned them inside.

Roy glanced around at the book-lined shelves and the accumulation of legal papers strewn across the desks and tables. "It appears business is brisk," Roy said, smiling.

Zach Marlowe stood unmoving a few steps behind him in the shadows, his hands folded in front.

"Yes?" Isaac Collier said, waiting to learn the purpose of the visit.

Roy shrugged. "Seems to me that with all your legal work—being so busy and all—you wouldn't have much time for mayoring, if you won the election, and I'm not saying you will win. But on the off-chance that you might, wouldn't it be better to let somebody who wants to work only at being mayor, be mayor? Better for you, better for the town. Better for everybody."

Collier's eyes narrowed. "What are you getting at? Speak plainly, sir."

"All right," Zach Marlowe said now and stepped up out of the shadow. "Here it is: if you were to quit this race today because of your law practice, my boss, Mr. Granger here, would be in a position to throw a heap of legal business your way. An awful lot. Enough to make you the biggest law office in West Texas and a very wealthy man." He looked over at Auguste Philippe sitting behind his desk and listening closely. "Your partner too. Believe me, folks around here would understand. All you have to do is write out a withdrawal notice now and we'll have it printed in *The Express* tonight."

Isaac Collier looked disdainfully at Roy, drew a deep breath and slowly shook his head. "So that's it," he said. "Your old man thinks his lapdog Mobley can't win, even with all these street-bullies in town, so he sends his errand-boy to buy me off. To bribe me out of it. Sorry. I'm not interested. We'll just have to let the voters decide. Good day, gentlemen."

"You're making a mistake," Zach Marlowe said softly.

"No," Collier said. "You are. Get out of my office, both of you. And don't come back."

Roy Granger reacted like a match to blasting powder. He reached back and brought his arm up in the same backhanded sweeping motion with which his father had struck him earlier, and hit Collier with a resounding *thwack*. Then he cracked him on the jaw with a hard-knuckled fist, sprawling him into the desk, and knocking over an oil-lamp, sending it crashing to the floor. "I'll kill you if you don't write it," Roy said.

Now Philippe lunged from his chair in an exclamation of shocked protest and reached for the gun belts hanging from an oak coat rack behind him. But he was too clumsy and too slow. In one blinding instant, a black-handled Colt appeared in Zach Marlowe's right hand, its hammer cocked. Marlowe squeezed the trigger and hit Philippe in the left side of his chest. He crumpled, face ghastly with agony, and fell, dead before his shoulders touched the floor.

Roy Granger stood staring down at Collier and shaking his head. "I didn't want this," he said. "You should've taken my offer. Now it's too late. Your friend there bleeding all over that fancy rug made sure of that."

"What have you done?" Collier gasped, frozen against the front panel of the desk, his arms outstretched. "Don't you realize you'll both hang for this?"

Roy placed his index finger in a vertical position over his lips, indicating that he wanted Isaac Collier to be silent. "No. We won't. But no matter what happens, you won't be here to see it. The election is over. And you've been outvoted."

Roy unsheathed his revolver and cocked the hammer, the barrel pointing downward at the floor. He raised the weapon, extended his arm and fired a shot point-blank into Isaac Collier's chest. Collier went down with a heavy heave. With fiendish calm, Roy fired once more. The gun barrel smoked; Collier's legs twitched. Blood seeped through his shirt and thinly trickled from his lips. But Collier never felt the second bullet. He was already dead.

Marlowe quickly placed a revolver near the hand of each dead man. Then he sat down in a high-backed, velvet-covered chair, crossed his legs, took out his tobacco pouch and papers, rolled two cigarettes, lit both, handed one to Roy, and calmly waited.

The crowd soon arrived, followed by Noble Caulder with a shotgun in his hands. He did not need it. The two men calmly and peacefully handed over their pistols and told their tale for everyone to hear.

It was brief. They had been invited to a meeting to discuss Collier's withdrawal from the mayor's race and were forced to suddenly defend themselves from an attack by the two law partners who became enraged by the knowledge of Collier's impending defeat, and drew down on them. Zach Marlowe and Roy Granger had discharged their weapons only as a last resort in defense of their lives, they claimed.

Noble Caulder was not deceived, but knew he had no choice except to return their weapons to them and let them go about their business. There was no one to dispute their version of the killings. The only other witnesses to the shootings were lying dead on floor.

Chapter Four

The morning sun cast a fresh day across the Pecos. News of the deaths of law partners Collier and Philippe spread rapidly throughout the county. By mid-morning, Manolo had brought word to William Hart.

"This not good, *mi amigo*," said Manolo after relaying the news of the murders to Will. "Big trouble coming with *Señor* Granger and the *pistoleros* in long coats."

"I know," said Will, grimly. He was thinking of his friend Noble Caulder, and he felt a pang in his chest. He was worried.

Nothing like this had happened in Enterprise in recent memory. Last year, two drunken saddle-tramps had shot it out in front of Spanish Red's, over a woman. A bystander had been grazed by a stray bullet, but both gunmen had missed. While the two duelers were in jail, the townspeople laughed when the woman ran off with a dry-goods peddler.

But this was different. This threatened everyone. The town's soul was at stake. The Grangers wanted something badly and now proved they would do anything to get it—even murder.

By six o'clock, there were almost a dozen buggies and buckboards parked in front of the church yard. Despite the recent violence and premonition of trouble in the air, the mood in town this evening was festive.

People had traveled many miles to attend the reception for Dr. and Mrs. Bransom. Isolation on the plains made any social event worth the hours of uncomfortable travel required. Fellowship and entertainment, society versus loneliness, called to everyone and welcomed everybody into the church hall, regardless of differences between backgrounds or faith.

Most folks around the region knew Doc Bransom, who had helped bring many new lives into this part of West Texas. As the occasion was large, many guests wore their finery. Thad Miller, the town blacksmith, and his wife were there in their Sunday best; the Sanders family, from up near Horseneck Pass, had driven down with a grand vanilla-frosted cake that Ruth Sanders, a stout pleasant-faced woman, had baked for the occasion; Mr. and Mrs. Oakley came in from Cross Creek; Jed Pugh, the proprietor of the tonsorial parlor and barber shop, had come; Lucas and Julianne Madison were there, with Julianne now mixing the lemonade in a big punchbowl; of course, Pilar and Manolo were there too, and all the West Texas members of the Society of Friends. Even Lobo the tawny-haired dog was welcomed at the affair, trailing Billy and sniffing around to locate anything worth gobbling.

Will noticed that the only friend who was not there yet was Noble Caulder; he guessed that Noble was busy keeping a watchful eye on the streets.

While the musicians took a break, Will mingled with other guests. He went over to the food tables, bounteous with treasures of potluck brought by the guests, and fixed himself a plate of grilled beef, fried chicken, corn-on-the-cob and apple pie. He sat eating and chatting, watching Beth happily serve refills of coffee and talking with guests. She was wearing a new gingham dress with a button-down bodice and white lace trim at the collar and wrists. The dress featured a billowing skirt that gathered at the waist, and Will admired the graceful contour from across the room.

With her black hair cascading down her back, her deep-brown eyes sparkling, her face radiant with thought and compassion, Will imagined her as Helen of Troy. Hers, he felt, was a face to launch a thousand ships. Even after all this time, she was still the most striking woman he had ever seen.

Finishing his plate, he set his fork down and walked over to her. "Are you enjoying the party?" he asked.

"Oh, yes, very much." She smiled. "It's wonderful to see so many friends and neighbors. What about you? Are you enjoying it?"

"Sure am." He jokingly tugged at his buttoned collar with black string tie, and smiled. "How about a dance?"

"There's no music."

"I'll fix that." He went over and whispered to the musicians, seated beside their instruments.

There were five of them, all in dark suits and with their hair slicked-down, each holding an instrument—a banjo, a fiddle, a bass fiddle, a guitar and an accordion. They stood up at once and played one of Beth's favorite romantic songs called *In the Moonlit Meadow*.

"You remembered," Beth blushed.

A number of other couples joined Will and Beth on the dance floor, including the guests of honor.

"You're the prettiest girl in here," Will said as they swayed to the music. Beth's right hand clutched his left and her head rested on his shoulder. "For that matter, in all of Texas."

"And you're the handsomest fellow," she told him. "Oh, Will, do you think we'll be as happy as the Bransom's are after fifty years?"

"Without a doubt," Will said, looking into her eyes and lightly touching a rosy cheek.

After that song ended, the tempo and the volume rose. The musicians began to play a medley of rousing Texas tunes. The guitar twanged and the banjo plinked, the accordion puffed and the fiddles fiddled; they cut loose and began rocking the hall and kicking off the quadrille—that square dance with intricate figures—and playing circle and reel dances accompanied by foot stomping and knee slapping. Everyone, including the children, joined in.

"*I laid out in the shade,*'" the singer warbled, "*'I gave her every dime I made. What else could a poor boy do? Who'll rock the cradle when you're gone, when you're gone? I'll rock the cradle and I'll sing a song. I'll rock the cradle when you're gone.*'"

The singer, also the caller, directed the dancing, adding rhyming lines which he made up as he went along. The hall resounded with the din of dancing feet and the ring of clapping hands.

After a few minutes, Will took a breather. He left Beth mingling with ladies from the church, sat down and sipped a cup of lemonade. He looked around for his son; Billy was not in the hall. Then it occurred to Will that he had not seen him for some time. Knowing the mischief little boys can get into, Will decided he better go look for him. And he had heard that the preacher had some announcements to make soon.

Will went out onto the lamp-lit porch and looked around. The evening was warm, and in the distance he marveled at the Pecos sunset that silhouetted the small town with a palette of pink and purple and silver streaked with a background of deep rich gold. Walking down the wooden steps, he quickened his pace when he heard grunts and groans. Turning the corner of the church building, he nearly tripped over Billy and another boy tussling in the grass.

The boy was rolling around on the ground, fighting with Tommy Miller, Thad's son. They were wrestling each other while the whining dog leaped around as if wanting to join the scuffle.

Will reached down, grabbed both boys by their shirts, separated them, and yanked them up. He held them apart, each red-faced nine-year-old scowling at the other. The dog pranced toward Will, wagging its tail and jumping at him.

"What in the thunder is going on here?" Will said.

"Nothing," Billy told him, catching a glance at Tommy.

"Nothing? We're at church, at an anniversary party, everyone's having a good time, and you're out here in a fight with one of your best friends? I'll ask again. What's this about?" He released his grip on the two and looked back and forth between them.

Billy suddenly gushed, "He started hitting Lobo and I told him to stop but he wouldn't and I yelled at him to stop and Lobo was barking and he started chasing him and then I grabbed him to make him stop and—"

Tommy Miller interrupted him. "That dog is ill-mannered. Why, he stole food right off my plate, Mr. Hart." The boy then continued in a torrent of his own, "And he kept following me everywhere and I told him to go away but he didn't listen and then Billy started yelling and the dog started growling and trying to snap my feet and I had to—"

"That's enough!" Will cut them off. "I want you both to listen carefully." He crouched down between them. "Fighting doesn't solve anything. It only makes problems worse. If I hadn't come and the two of you knocked each other senseless, would that change what happened with the dog? Would it prevent it from happening again?"

Neither boy said anything.

"Well?" Will asked. "Would it?"

"No, Mr. Hart," Tommy Miller said, looking away.

"No, Pa," Billy said, looking down at the ground.

"Good. You two are friends. And friends don't hurt one another. I want you each to apologize and then shake hands. Like friends. Like men."

"Do I have to, Pa?"

"Yes. You have to. It's the right thing."

"I'm sorry," Billy said and stuck his hand out.

"Me too," Tommy said and clasped it.

Neither of them looked at the other.

"All right," Will said. "Tuck your shirttails in, fix your hair, and go inside and get something to eat." He glared at the dog, which had started after them. "Oh, no, not you, Lobo." With an extended hand, he gently tapped the dog on the rump and said, "Now, stay."

The dog lay down with its back legs stretched out, panting and watching after the boys as they both laughed and ran up the steps to the fellowship hall.

Will returned to the party. When the music stopped, the guests clapped and the caller bellowed in his loud tone, "Would everyone gather round. Preacher Cullen has some important announcements he wants to make."

The preacher climbed up on a chair next to the musicians, and held up his arms, requesting quiet.

Will motioned Billy over to him and they went and stood next to Beth. Will took her hand.

"Friends," he said when the droning subsided. "I'll make this brief. I know everyone wants to get back to this terrific party."

"Yeah, no sermon tonight, please preacher!" a voice chuckled. Someone else whistled.

The preacher grinned. "Thank you all for coming. I know it was a long journey for many of you. First, I want to wish Frank and Emma Bransom our best wishes and many happy returns on this, their fiftieth wedding anniversary. God bless you both," he said looking down at the elderly couple. "You are an inspiration to us all."

Everyone clapped and a score of voices shouted, "Happy Anniversary!"

Will whispered to Beth, "That's going to be us in forty years." She wrinkled her nose and squeezed his hand.

The preacher's smile now disappeared. "Second," he said, "and on a much more somber note: I'd like to ask for a moment of silent prayer and reflection regarding the violent and untimely deaths of our friends Isaac Collier and Auguste Philippe. May the Lord take their souls to His bosom, and may He comfort the widows and families." He continued in a rising crescendo, "And because the laws of men are powerless here, may He mete out divine justice to the perpetrators of this vile crime."

"Amen," several voices rose in agreement.

Everyone bowed their heads.

After a moment, Preacher Cullen continued. "And third," he said, "it's my privilege to announce to you that, as of this afternoon, we have a new candidate for mayor on the democrat ticket. He will save Enterprise five days from now by winning an election landslide: Sheriff Noble Caulder, the People's Choice!"

The entire hall broke out in prolonged applause. Noble Caulder had not arrived yet, but the preacher said the sheriff was on official business and that he would stop by the party later in the evening.

Noble Caulder was well-liked and highly respected. He was their perfect choice, their true champion, a better choice even than Isaac Collier had been. For he was the one man they knew could stand up for Enterprise and prevail against the power of Sam Granger.

Will was the only person who did not applaud. The announcement caught him by surprise and made him feel like he'd been punched in the stomach. *Darn you, Noble,* he thought. *Why did you have to ruin a perfectly good party? Are you looking to commit suicide? Sam Granger will never let you win. He'll assassinate you, just like Collier. Why stick your neck out any further for this town? They've never done anything for you.*

While afraid for his friend's safety, Will would not allow his fear to turn unfair. He understood Noble's reason: the oath. What the man had sworn. Not to the badge or to the town; that could be ignored. Only his word to himself counted. Noble had gone and done this stupid thing for honor. So he could sleep at night and look himself in the face come morning. If he couldn't, life wasn't worth living in the first place.

And, Will knew, Noble did it because he hated the arrogance of power; any power, all power. He'd always despised the notion of different laws for rich and poor, white men and red men, strong and weak. For Noble Caulder, there was only one law: right justice. He would apply it equally to everyone or die in the attempt. Otherwise his world could make no sense.

Will put his arm around Beth's waist and pulled her close. She was applauding with enthusiasm along with everyone else. "It's no good," he said, shaking his head. "No good at all."

Noting the queer sound in his voice, she quit clapping. "Why? What do you mean?"

"What do I mean? Look what happened to—"

Crash! Without notice, the double-doors to the fellowship hall burst open, jarring the whole hall. The applause died. A commotion was coming from the other end of the room. Everyone turned to look.

Half a dozen regulators, led by Zach Marlowe, had come into the hall. Standing side by side in a line, in long dusters and black hats, they grinned at the astonished crowd, their demeanor fitting their purpose—to intimidate. Two of them had election flyers in their hands. This pair began shouldering their way through the guests and roughly distributing their bills, in much the same way as Will had witnessed the day before.

"We heard there was a big shindig," Zach Marlowe said, "and figured why not join the fun? Free eats and drinks, and pretty girls."

He went over and took a piece of beef off a platter, sat on the table and put one leg up while he ate. His heavy boot left a dirt streak on the white table-linen. "It's good you folks are together; makes my job easy. You need to forget about voting for that broken-down sheriff. Aaron Mobley is your man. That's tonight's message."

Spurred, booted, and packing heavy guns low down on their hips, the two passing out the handbills now began knocking over dishes and smashing cups and plates on the floor. One dumped the entire punchbowl out over a man's shoes, then heaved the fluted bowl against the wall, shattering it and spraying glass around. His partner shoved his way past everyone to the musicians, picked up the banjo, ripped off its strings and smashed the instrument against the floor. When the owner-musician jumped up shouting, the regulator hit him with it on the side of the head, knocking him backward onto a chair.

Preacher Cullen hurried to confront Zach Marlowe. "How dare you and your ruffians enter a house of God with arms and violence. Leave our town and our people in peace, Satan. Go, I tell you!"

Zach Marlowe winked. He picked up another slice of beef, chewed it, closed his eyes savoring the taste, swallowed, stood up and took hold of the preacher by his frock coat. He threw him to the floor. "Now, that's downright un-Christian," he said. "Calling people names."

"Daddy!" Beth shouted. She ran to her father.

The crowd was petrified. No one said or did anything. The two regulators continued roughing up the guests and handing out flyers. Will moved toward Beth and her father, bent down and eased the preacher to his feet. Then he faced Zach Marlowe.

"Look, Marlowe, you've made your point, stated your political choice. You've wrecked a fine anniversary party. Feel good? Now, why don't you leave us in peace? Like my father-in-law asked."

Marlowe eyed Will, blinking his steely, gray eyes several times. "Ah, well. If it ain't Mr. Concerned Citizen himself." He noticed Beth. She was holding the preacher's arm and Zach Marlowe looked her up and down with a leer. "This sweet thing's your wife?" he asked, stroking his long mustache. "You're not quite the dumb farmer I thought." He grinned and winked at Beth.

Will's muscles tightened. "Why don't you and your *election-eers* leave now?" he said in a cool, easy manner.

Marlowe made his right hand into a fist and returned Will's request with a hit in the mouth, cutting his lower lip. Neither raising his hands nor backing off, Will continued staring without expression. Their glances locked steadily, each man taking measure of the other.

"Leave," Will said. "Take your gunmen. There's nothing here for you."

Marlowe stared back at him a moment. His face twitched and then he hit Will again, this time with the back of his left hand. He caught him on the nose with his knuckles, drawing blood from one nostril. Still Will did not move.

"Hitting is a waste," Will told him, wiping blood from his nose and lips. "I'm not going to fight you. There's no good reason to fight."

"There's her," Marlowe smirked, making a sweeping motion with his head toward Beth.

"No. There's a hundred witnesses here. And you'd have to kill me first."

"I can do that." His tone was provoking. Marlowe struck Will once more, this time full on the mouth, again with his closed right fist. Once more Will took it without backing away. His head jerked back from the force of the blow but he remained standing on the same mark.

Marlowe raised his fist again, but Beth now thrust herself between the two, arms outstretched. Shielding Will, she tried to push Zach Marlowe away. "Leave him alone, you filthy brute! You can't get away with this, let me tell you. Not when Sheriff Caulder finds out!"

The regulator grinned. "Ain't you the hot tamale? You got more fire than this here husband of yours, girl. I *am* going to see you one of these days."

"You revolt me," Beth said, spitting the words, her hands clenched at her sides.

Marlowe laughed. "Who knew," he said to Will, "that you'd need a skirt for protection? What kind of man hides behind a woman?"

Several of the *pistoleros* guffawed.

Marlowe inclined his head toward the door. "Let's go," he said to his men. Then, loudly, "You people better remember what I said. If not, well, pray you don't have to find out what'll happen."

And then they were gone. Everybody gathered around Will and the preacher while Beth wiped Will's face with a cloth napkin, gently dabbing the deep gash on his lower lip. "Go get the sheriff," she commanded to men standing nearby.

"No," Will said. "It's over. There's nothing the sheriff can do now. He'll find out about it soon enough."

"Nothing he can do?" Beth said, angrily. "He can arrest them! Put them in jail where they belong. That's what he can do."

"No," Will said again. "Leave it. Don't go stirring them up. I don't want anyone else getting hurt."

"Will is right," the preacher said to his daughter. "Those are cruel and vengeful men. When the time comes, the sheriff will know how to deal with them."

Some guests began setting up overturned chairs, cleaning the debris and picking broken glass off the floor and tables. Many of the women clung to their men and cast anxious looks toward the door. The children huddled next to their parents, round-eyed and silent.

Will felt a tug on his sleeve. It was Billy. His eyes were filled with tears, although he was trying to hold them back.

"Everything's okay now, Billy," Will said gently, reaching to put a comforting hand on his son's shoulder. But the boy pulled away. "What's wrong?" asked Will.

"Pa," he said. "How could you let him hit you like that? Why didn't you do something? Why didn't you fight back? You could beat him. I know you could."

"Remember what I told you before? About Lobo and Tommy?" His son's shame pained him more than any of Zach Marlowe's blows had. "It wouldn't have changed anything. It could've gotten someone hurt."

Tears slid down the boy's cheeks. "How could you let him beat you in front of everybody? How could you not hit him back?"

"Sometimes things aren't what they seem," Will said. He sighed, and looked achingly at his son.

"Why don't you wear a gun, like everybody else?" Billy retorted. "You're the only father who never wears a gun." It was an accusation.

"Not the only one. And you know our beliefs. Violence is wrong. Guns make it too easy. There are better ways to deal with conflict besides fighting."

"Your Pa is right," Preacher Cullen told his grandson. "Listen to him. If we believe something, then we have to stand up for it, whether or not standing up for it is hard."

"I hate our beliefs," Billy said, red-faced and looking up tearfully at Will. "And I hate you."

"Billy!" Beth shouted as the boy stalked off. "Come back here. Don't you ever talk to your father like that." She started after him but Will held her wrist.

"Let him go," he said. "It's all right. I know how he feels. He'll get over it."

"I won't put up with him saying such things to you," Beth said. "I won't!" She began to cry.

Will wrapped both arms around her. "Don't cry. He doesn't mean it. Come on," he said. "Let's help to clean up this mess in here."

Over at Spanish Red's, Roy Granger sat drinking tequila. He was hunched over the end of the long, polished bar, his foot tapping the lower brass rail, and watching disinterestedly as four men played poker at a nearby table.

The hands on the big wooden clock on the wall behind the bar crept toward eight o'clock. Usually Noble Caulder would have stopped in by now making his rounds. But Roy had been waiting for almost an hour and was in a foul mood because of it.

If Noble Caulder didn't show soon, Roy would have to go find *him*. He kept one eye on the doors, hoping. He wanted to get this over with.

In the background, piano music tinkled softly. On a request, the sandy-whiskered piano man in a white shirt and satiny red vest fingered the keys to Stephen Foster's *Beautiful Dreamer.* A couple of lanky cowpunchers with mugs of beer lounged at the bar, and another sat drinking at a small table in the corner. There was a strapping yellow-haired girl in a red dress—all Red's girls wore trademark red dresses—standing behind the poker players.

Business was slow tonight and so the painted-face girl stayed there, her skirt swishing as she moved from one player to another. Every so often the winner of a pot would slip her a coin and she'd refill their drinks. Then she'd smile, bat her eyes, and plant a kiss on the top of the winner's head. The others at the table would hoot and holler, and the girl would be slipped another coin.

Jorge Velasquez, a Spaniard from Madrid with pumpkin-colored hair—Spanish Red himself—was behind the bar tonight. He was keeping his distance from Roy Granger. He had glimpsed his temper before and had no wish to become the object of his anger.

"Another tequila," Roy called out. He held up his shot glass and wiggled it in the air.

Jorge Velasquez hurried over and poured the shot. Roy swigged it and then banged his glass down. The barman poured another.

"Anybody seen that old man Caulder tonight?" Roy said. "Or is he hiding up at that holier-than-thou *soiree*?"

The barman shrugged. No one else said anything.

Roy drank the shot and wiped his mouth with the back of his hand. Then called again, louder this time, "Anybody seen Caulder?" and with a curse ordered the piano man to stop his playing.

When no one answered, Roy picked up his shot glass and threw it at the poker players. It banged off the table, knocking some cards to the floor, and barely missed hitting one of the four men.

"I asked a question," Roy said. "You idiots got ears and tongues?"

"Hey, come on, Roy," the girl said sweetly, trying to calm him down. "Don't be like that." She knew him too.

"Shut up, Lucille. Red! Get over here and bring me more tequila."

The barman brought over a shot glass and a bottle. Before he filled it, Roy picked the glass up and again hurled it at the poker game, this time hitting one of the players in the arm. The man slapped his cards on the table and leaped up.

"Sit down," Roy ordered him, drawing his pistol and pointing it at him.

The man held out his hands to his side and sat down slowly. "Listen, mister. We don't want trouble. All we want is to—"

Roy turned and aimed the gun toward the back of the room. He squeezed off a shot and broke a glass lamp over the staircase, shattering it into a thousand shivering splinters.

"*Señor*, please," Jorge Velasquez said. "Do not shoot guns in Spanish Red's place."

"Quiet, greaser," Roy said. He fired again, hitting a second lamp on the wall beside the banister.

Jorge Velasquez thought that if Roy was drunk it did not show in his shooting. His aim was much too good.

The cowboy at the corner table got up, inched along the far wall, came around and eased out the swinging doors. Roy Granger disregarded him.

"I'll shoot this place to tar-nation and back," Roy yelled.

"*Como que?*" the barman said. *"No. Por favor."*

Roy fired a third time and struck the huge mirror behind the bar. He laid the revolver on the wooden bar in front of him and motioned to the barman for another shot glass. Jorge Velasquez gave him one and lifted the bottle to pour a drink. Roy grabbed it away from him. "Get lost," he said, pouring out the amber liquid himself. He stood there in silence drinking the tequila and watching, waiting.

He did not have to wait long. Five minutes later the saloon doors swung inward and Noble Caulder stepped through, tall and broad, carrying his shotgun. He saw Roy, saw the gun on the bar, and said, "You shooting the place up, Granger?"

"Yep," Roy said.

"You are just asking for trouble, aren't you boy? You drunk?" Noble asked.

"Nope. Taking target practice." He looked over at Jorge Velasquez. "I'll pay the damages." Roy plucked two twenty-dollar gold pieces from his shirt pocket, stacked them on the bar and turned over an empty shot glass on top of them.

"Roy," Noble said from the other end of the bar. "Slide that pistol down here. Nice and easy."

"Okay, Sheriff Caulder," Roy said. "Anything you say."

He spun the pistol down the bar's length. Noble picked it up and stuck it in his belt.

"Come along with me," Noble said.

"Where to?" Roy asked.

"To my office. There's a nice cell with your name on it."

"What's the charge?"

"Disturbing the peace, for starters."

"Okay, Sheriff Caulder."

He came around the corner of the bar and sauntered up to Noble. "You gonna shackle me with hand-irons?"

"Look, boy, as long as you come quietly and peacefully, I won't have to."

"I'll come peaceful-like," Roy said. "Won't give you a bit of trouble. That's a promise. Would you like a drink before we go, Sheriff? I'll buy. Whatever you like."

Noble stared at him curiously. Something seemed odd. "Never mind that, Granger. Let's go."

They went out and walked up main street together. Noble was drawn-faced and tired, but alert. He carried the shotgun cradled in his left arm while Roy walked quietly on his right. Neither man spoke. As they neared the sheriff's office they could see a lone lamplight flickering in the window. Noble stopped in front of the door, dug into his pocket with his right hand and took out a jangling ring of keys.

At that moment, movement caught the corner of his eyes. Four figures in long coats stepped up out of the dark on either side of the walkway. In a fleeting glance, Noble recognized one of them as Zach Marlowe. As the sheriff turned, Roy swiped at the pistol in his belt.

Noble reacted by driving the butt of the shotgun into Roy's shoulder. Before he could heft it, there was a blast. Noble heard the *bam!* of a pistol and felt the burn of a bullet sear deep in his back.

Lurching forward, the shotgun tumbled loose from Noble's stretching fingers. He grasped for the revolver strapped to his chest, but was too late. Roy Granger had the pistol out of Noble's belt. He cocked the hammer and fired into his gut, moving back as the sheriff crashed onto the wooden planks of the sidewalk.

Legs drawn up to his stomach and bleeding heavily, Noble clawed at the ground and tried to crawl forward to reach the barrel of the shotgun. Roy put a boot-heel into his neck and held him still.

"I told you, old man. We own this town."

"Will…" Noble gasped, struggling for air. "Will…"

Roy glanced at Zach Marlowe who was still holding his own smoking revolver, and nodded. Then they emptied the remaining slugs of their six-shooters into the sheriff's chest. The lawman went limp. He did not speak or move again.

Will's ears perked at the sound of gunfire. It came from the direction of town. Two he counted, the rest were too close together to tally. Joshua McGrath burst into the church hall, trembling, breathing hard. The spindly freight office clerk had worked late this night on some record-keeping and had been about to leave the office when he saw what happened to Sheriff Caulder through his window. Waiting until after the shooters had vanished, he ran as fast as he could to the church to fetch Doc Bransom.

"Where's the doc?" he queried Preacher Cullen. "We need him quick. The sheriff's been shot."

The preacher summoned Doc Bransom, and the three gathered quietly in the corner.

"Please, don't tell nobody it was me told you," Joshua McGrath whispered. "If they find out they'll kill me sure. That poor sheriff—doing him the way they done! He called the name 'Will' with his dying breath, he did. Your son-in-law I'd guess," he said looking at Preacher Cullen. "They are—were—friends. Oh, doc the sheriff needs you badly."

People were already leaving in their buckboards and buggies, and the preacher and doctor did not want to panic them at this hour or frighten the children any more than they had already been this evening. They said nothing to anyone, quickly found Will, took him aside and made McGrath tell him his story of the cowardly cold-blooded ambush.

McGrath's report had paralyzed him. A clammy sweat came to his face and the hollow of his hands. A horrible, sickening pressure oppressed his heart. Quietly, Will asked several questions. Then he went over to Manolo Sanchez. "I need you to do something. Something important."

"Si," said the *Segundo*. "Anything."

"Take Beth and Billy home, Manolo. And watch over them. I may not be back for a while." His face was gray. "I have an errand to run."

"But why, at this hour? What has happened?"

"My own business. That I should have taken care of before now."

"Do you want me to come with you, *hombre?* I might be able to help."

"No, man. But thank you. What you'll do for me at home is *muy importante.* Beth will be worried when I say I'm leaving. I will not tell her the truth. So I need you and Pilar there with her when she learns the truth. I'll speak to her now. Then you take her and my boy. Whatever you do, don't act nervous. But watch them. Like a mother hen. *Entiendes?"*

"*Si.* There is no problem. But, those *pistoleros* that came here! It's bad for you, eh?"

"*Malo,"* Will said.

"I'm sorry."

"So am I."

He went and spoke to Beth and he could see Manolo watching him.

"Can't you tell me why and where you're going?" she asked, searching his face for a sign.

"You'll know soon enough."

"You're frightening me, Will. Does it have to do with those men that were here? Is it Noble? Please, tell me. We've never had secrets from each other."

That you know of, he thought, sadly. "Do you trust me?" he asked.

"Of course I trust you, but…"

"No buts, then. Trust me. I love you. I'll see you later." He kissed her cheek, nodded once to Manolo and left the church.

Under the light of a full moon, Will and Doc Bransom left the church yard and strode briskly up main street. Up ahead they could see the lights of lanterns and torches; a small crowd of about a dozen, murmuring in low voices, huddled about on the boardwalk in front of the sheriff's office and in the street.

The crowd fell silent as they saw Will and the doctor approach. Will's heart beat faster as he pushed his way through the throng. When he came up to the sheriff's office, he saw the reason for the commotion. Will stood with a face as gray and still as stone.

Death had met Will's gaze many times in his life, but never like this. Horror clenched at his soul. Sadness struck at his heart. And he became enraged as never before.

Chapter Five

Four townsmen were standing directly over Noble Caulder. William Hart thrust them aside to let Doc Bransom through, but there was nothing a doctor could do for the sheriff now.

The killers had positioned the body so that Noble was seated upright in the rocking chair on the porch in front of the sheriff's office, like he was taking a nap. The brown Stetson was turned sideways on his head and the open shotgun lay across his lap. Both shells had been taken out and shoved into his mouth. His silver star had been ripped off his vest and was used to pin a piece of parchment paper to his chest which had been bloodied by the cluster of bullet holes. The paper was a handbill that said, ELECT MOBLEY, MOBLEY FOR MAYOR. At the bottom of the handbill was mockingly scribbled in lead pencil, *"I QUIT!"*

Will stood looking down at his friend. A lump formed deep in his throat. Their friendship—they were closer than brothers—had lasted since the war. It should not have ended now, not here; like this. *This blood,* Will thought, *is on my hands.* His refusal to help had killed Noble as much as if he had pulled the trigger himself. Yet, Will had not stayed away from the trouble. So what was the point in refusing? He'd been half into the Granger problem and half out. But Noble Caulder was all dead.

He should've shown loyalty, at whatever cost. How could the cost have seemed too high? Will owed Noble his life. Had his love for a woman and his idyllic family life turned him selfish? Now it was too late.

Gently, Will removed the sheriff's silver badge, wiped it against his shirt, and put it in his pocket. He tore the note off the body, crumpled it up and threw it into the street, where a gust of west wind took it. Then, he took away the shotgun shells, tossed them on the ground, and gently closed Noble's mouth. He lifted the shotgun, snapped it closed and stood it up against the window. He placed the Stetson, which he turned frontward, over his friend's face, as if to shield him from the bright light of the lanterns.

Then Will bowed his head, and wiped his blurred eyes. He placed a hand on his dead friend's shoulder, and whispered, "I'm so sorry, Colonel." He stood there silently for a moment more, until a slight tremble shook all his muscles at once. He knew what he had to do. It wouldn't bring Noble back. But it might help him rest easier.

Will drew the pearl-handled Colt .45 Peacemaker from the holster. He cracked the cylinder and saw that the revolver was still fully loaded. He slipped the pistol back inside the leather and slid it in and out, making sure it was loose and did not stick. Then he removed the shoulder harness from the body and strapped the rig across his own chest. He turned to the crowd and asked, "Anyone seen Granger and Marlowe?"

A short, round man with mutton-chop whiskers came through and up the steps onto the porch. It was Jeff Sykes, who worked for Western Union. "I have," he said. He looked at the body and shook his head. "Sheriff Noble was a friend."

"Where are they?" Will asked.

Before he answered, somebody hollered, "Sykes, no!" The man called out, "Marlowe swears he'll burn Enterprise to the ground if anybody tries anything."

"That won't happen," Will said.

"The sheriff is dead," someone else in the crowd yelled. "If they can kill him, they can kill any of us. There's no one to stop Sam Granger now."

"I've got to try," Will said.

"You?" Sykes said. "Don't be a fool. You're just a farmer. They'll gun you down in a heartbeat."

"You said you knew where they were. Do you or don't you?"

"They're at Spanish Red's," Sykes told him. "I saw them in there not five minutes ago."

"You men, get him to the undertaker," Doc Bransom said, pointing to several of the onlookers. "And for heaven's sake, treat his body with respect." The doctor turned to Will and asked, "Are you okay, Will?"

Will said nothing, but started off down the street.

Sykes and Doc Bransom hollered after him in unison, "No, Will. Don't go!"

Will did not stop walking, did not turn around and did not answer.

Cautiously he approached the saloon. Before entering, he stood outside peering between the frosted-glass letters on the window: *Spanish Red's Saloon, Food & Drink.* Zach Marlowe and Roy Granger were inside, as were three regulators. There were no other customers.

He saw the red-skirted Lucille, a rose in her yellow hair, standing at the far end of the bar. She was beside Roy and squirming amid his rough handling. Jorge Velasquez was behind the bar. He had on a white apron. Everyone—except Velasquez and the girl—was laughing. Evidently, the wolves were not expecting any trouble from the sheep of this town.

Will walked in soundlessly. No one noticed him. He stood at the near end of the bar, with alert eyes keeping the action in front of him. He surveyed to see how the regulators were positioned and if they were sober. He watched Jorge Velasquez down at the other end, pouring a whiskey for Zach Marlowe. Marlowe's coat was off and Will could see the pair of black-butted pistols below his vest in their turned-around holsters. They looked like coiled cobras. He was rolling a cigarette.

When the barman noticed him, his eyes opened wide.

"Señor Will!" he said, staring at the revolver. He had never before seen Will carry a gun. No one in Enterprise had. "You should not be here like this—I mean, so late. I am...I am ready to close."

"Oh, no, you ain't," Roy Granger said with a half-sneer. "You're staying open all night for me and my friends and my girl here. Right, *honey?* And the night is still young." He pushed his face so hard against Lucille's that it made a red mark. She squealed and tried twisting away from him. But he held onto her.

"Hello, Jorge," Will said. *"Qué pasa, amigo?* I think you should go for a walk. Get some air. It's a nice night."

"He ain't going nowhere," Roy said. "Say, I remember you. From the store. With that Injun."

"What a memory," Will said.

"You," Zach Marlowe said to Will. He raised an eyebrow, straightened up and stared. He bolted down a shot of rye whiskey, and took a long draw on his cigarette. "Shouldn't you be praying someplace? I guess you ain't had enough teaching for one night."

"Go ahead, Jorge," Will said, ignoring Marlowe. "Leave. Take Lucille with you. Lucille, come down here to me. It's all right."

She wriggled away finally from Roy and hurried over to Will.

"Go," he said. Needing no persuasion, the girl left.

"Señor Hart," Jorge Velasquez said. "I would rather you took such a walk than me."

"Hart?" Zach Marlowe said. "William Hart?"

"My bartender ain't leaving," Roy said. "You can't come in here and—"

"Shut up, Roy," Zach Marlowe said, viciously. Something was on his mind. "William Hart. I know that name. If it's who I'm thinking."

"Go, Jorge," Will said. "Now."

Jorge Velasquez skipped quickly through the open lift-top of the bar and ducked out of the saloon. Roy Granger started to follow. Zach Marlowe stopped him.

"Forget the bartender. And keep your mouth shut, Roy. Hart," he repeated. "William Hart."

"Yes."

"The same name as a peace officer I heard tell of. Out of El Paso."

"Maybe it's a common name."

"You him?" Marlowe questioned.

"You figure it out," Will returned.

Marlowe noticed the look in Will's eyes and the Colt on his chest and felt a sudden menace. "You *are* him. You had me fooled back there in the church. Hiding behind a skirt that way." He grinned with a glint of mockery in his eyes, but there was no humor in it. "I've heard things about William Hart. Stories. Tall tales. Stuff that can't be true."

The other regulators were now paying attention. Even Roy Granger was listening.

"You like stories?" Will said. He was watching everyone, especially their hands. "Good. Let's talk. What stories do you mean? What did you hear?"

This was an old tactic that he learned from Noble Caulder— to put an enemy off guard. Make him talk, make him think about what you asked and what he was going to answer.

"I heard you were dead," Zach Marlowe told him, keeping his hands close to the butts of his guns, as if expecting a response greater than words.

"I was. I came back to life."

"I heard you were good friends with a piece of trash road agent named Cole Younger. He's rotting in prison now up North."

"I knew Cole for a while," Will said. "What else?"

"I heard the only law you ever cared about was your own. That you made your own law, with a .44. That you were lightning-fast with a six-shooter."

A small smile creased Will's lips. "Anything else?"

"I heard you put down two, three dozen men. And that you're a worse killer than the ones you sent to jail or to the grave."

Will nodded. "Now you know me."

"But none of that's true anymore, is it? You lost your nerve someplace. Being holed up with women and holy rollers has turned you soft, white-livered. You turned yellow, Hart."

"I've heard of you too, Marlowe," he said. "From Cole Younger, in fact."

"Is that right? What did that Missouri trash have to say?"

"He said you were a back-shooting *cobarde*. He said that the world would be better off without you."

"That a fact," Marlowe said curtly as he spat into the brass spittoon. It made a ringing sound.

Without taking his eyes from Marlowe, Will said, "I've come to take you and Granger to jail for the murder of Noble Caulder."

"You what?" Marlowe said, a baffled grin coming over his face. He was confused now as well as angry.

Will started walking toward him. He noted the gaunt cheeks and drooping mustache underneath the wide-rimmed black hat; as Marlowe swallowed, his dark stubble of beard moved up and down across the chords of his throat. His face was sullen and fierce.

Watching Will come toward him in full stride, Marlowe read his expression and his intention. His hands whipped for the onyx-handled pistols, and pulled both. At that same moment Roy Granger, sensing what was about to happen, bolted out around the corner of the bar and drew his gun.

Will went down to one knee just as Marlowe fired with twin spurts of lead and simultaneous *booms*; Roy's gun exploded at almost the same instant. The bullets whistled past his ear, splintering the front wall, sending bits of wood and tapestry flying.

Then the heavy Colt that was once Noble's leaped forth in Will's right hand and *bang!* The .45 spoke. He fired at Marlowe, smoke curling from the muzzle. The round clipped Marlowe in the side of the neck; he reeled and dropped, knocking aside two chairs. Will's second shot struck Roy Granger, square in the chest, sending him crashing into the bar and falling in a heap. Will had not fired a pistol in years, yet the nerves and muscles of his hands had retained their memory. He'd always been one of the best on the frontier at making a shot count.

Marlowe jerked the trigger of the gun in his left hand as he toppled over onto his right side. The bullet flew four feet wide. Will wheeled and threw a glance at the grave-faced regulators and then looked at Roy. The young Granger's body was lifeless; the first bullet had finished him. Now he stood erect and walked over to Marlowe.

Zach Marlowe was on his back lying parallel to the bar with one leg tucked underneath him. Dark blood from the big .45-caliber neck-wound soaked Marlowe's yellow scarf and seeped down onto his vest. His eyes were glazed, the pupils dilated; he was staring up at the ceiling.

With Noble's pistol hanging in his hand, Will checked the other regulators again. All of them were motionless, stunned by the outcome of the fight, knowing how deadly it might be for any of them to make a significant move. This farmer-man, Hart, had shaken them. In less than five seconds he had destroyed a dangerous gunfighter along with the son of Sam Granger. With two shots.

"Nobody moves," Will told the regulators. "Take those pistols out butt-first and lay them on the bar." Standing over Marlowe, he kicked away the pair of black revolvers.

"You can't kill us all," one *pistolero* said. "Somebody will get you."

"Maybe," Will said. "But *you* die first. Now, *take out those guns.* Slide them down the bar. All the way."

The three regulators decided to do what they were told.

Now Will squatted down and leaned close to Zach Marlowe, whose life was draining with each second. With his left hand, he reached in his pocket and brought out Noble's silver star.

"In the name of the State of Texas, I am placing you under arrest for the murder of Noble Caulder," Will told him. "Remember the name: Noble Caulder. Cavalry Colonel, Confederate States of America, United States Marshal, Sheriff of Enterprise; the best man who ever walked this earth. Remember his name while you rot in jail or burn in hell, whatever comes first."

He stood and drew a deep breath. There was no sound except the ticking of the clock. Relief overcame him and in a moment he let his guard down. From his rear, a long barrel of a Winchester appeared from above the swinging doors of the saloon. Will's keen eye caught the movement in a piece of broken mirror on the back of the bar. Instantly, he pivoted as the shot rang out. Will felt a sudden sharp crack in the back of his skull. His body jerked forward and his pistol tumbled from his fingers. A wave of pain flashed across his face. He felt the heat of the bullet and tasted blood. The floor spun; his body sagged. He reached for the bar, but fell short, falling onto his stomach beside Zach Marlowe.

He tried getting up but did not have the strength. For a fleeting instant he imagined being in bed beside Beth. *Oh Beth*, he thought. *What have I done? I'm so sorry.* Then he glimpsed a dusty boot, a tarnished spur, and the hem of a trail coat. But the dim light in Spanish Red's quickly faded to black and Will Hart ceased thinking any thoughts at all.

When he came to, Will was draped over a saddle bouncing up and down to the pace of the horse, his head throbbing with pain, his hands tied behind his back. The bullet had grazed the flesh of Will's head from the side, but had not entered. His hair was matted with blood.

A tall horseman in a long coat holding a Winchester rode in front of him. Will had no recollection of seeing him before. Two of Marlowe's *pistoleros* from the saloon flanked him on either side; the one on his left was leading two more horses that carried the dead bodies of Roy Granger and Zach Marlowe. The third *pistolero* from the saloon rode behind him. They were on the north road leading from Enterprise toward the Pecos River. The night was dark and quiet.

The regulator on his right held the reins and led Will's horse along at a quick pace. Will listened to the clip-clop of the animals and tried to catch a glimpse of the stars to get a sense of where they were heading, but most of what he watched was the dark ground go by. He couldn't see the dust kicked up by the trotting hooves, but he could feel the bite of alkali stinging his nostrils. Scarcely an hour later, the riders approached a large *hacienda*, with windows shining like yellow squares on both the upper and lower floors.

Riflemen patrolled along a wood and barbed-wire fence that encircled the grounds around the house, and guards with shotguns manned the gate. The place looked to be a fortified camp. Will wondered who they were trying to protect themselves from. As they approached, two riflemen advanced to the foreground. A troop of six or eight others remained in the shadow. The gate creaked opened.

"Bad news," the lead *pistolero* said down to the gatekeeper. "I hate being the one to bring it."

The gatekeeper, with a Winchester in one hand and a lantern in the other, came over and looked curiously at Will. Will stared back. The man clucked his tongue and shook his head back and forth. He went and looked at the faces of the two bodies, groaned and shook his head again. "Dang, Ike! Better you tell the boss than me. He'll go crazy. Go ahead, Devlin. Go on up to the house. He's awake, working."

Leading Will's horse, they rode the hundred yards to the house and dismounted at a tie rail, tethering the animals. The man named Ike Devlin came over to Will and pushed him off the horse so that he landed on his head. "Get up," he said, shoving Will as he rose.

They went up the wooden steps of the long porch and to the big heavy double-doors. Hesitating for a moment, Devlin took a deep breath and banged the big iron knocker. A pretty woman in a silk robe, her long dark hair falling over her shoulders, opened the door. Will recognized her. It was Magdalena, the young Spanish woman with the parasol that he had seen on the arm of Sam Granger the other day in Noble's office.

"Evening, ma'am," Ike Devlin said. He took off his hat. "Sorry to bother you so late. But we have to see Mr. Granger. It's urgent. There's bad news."

She looked at Will without expression, without asking the news or saying anything. "Wait here." She left them on the porch and returned several minutes later. "He's in the library. He'll see you. Go down the hall, turn left and then left again. Go through the tall doors."

"Thank you, ma'am," Devlin said. He inclined his head toward the others and nodded. They all went down to see the boss.

Sam Granger was sitting in a high-backed leather chair behind a huge mahogany desk. The desk was littered with legal papers, architectural drawings, and maps of the southwestern United States and its territories. Every wall in the large room was lined, corner to corner, with books, from floor to ceiling. There were several tables made from trees—you could see the rings under the glossy varnish—and a long rectangular table in one corner surrounded by straight chairs. Several lamps, including one on the desk, lit the room, and Will could smell the oil burning mixed with the bittersweet odor of stale pipe tobacco.

Sam Granger was wearing a tan, banded-collar shirt with the sleeves rolled-up and the buttons open at the throat. He had on suspenders and a pair of wire-rimmed reading glasses. He looked up sharply when they entered. If he was surprised, his face did not show it.

The regulators stood awkwardly just inside the door of the big room, waiting. Devlin was in front and one regulator was on each side, holding Will by the elbow, like an escort. The fourth stood at his rear. Will's hands were still tightly bound behind his back.

"Where's Marlowe? Who is this man?" Granger queried.

The regulators looked at each other, and then Ike Devlin cleared his throat, "Umm, Mr. Granger, sir..."

"Well?" Sam Granger said after studying them a moment.

"Mr. Granger," Ike Devlin said. "Marlowe's dead, sir. And I hate to be the one to have to bring you—"

"Spit it out, man. I'm busy."

Devlin held his wide-brimmed black hat in front of him with both hands and looked down. Balding in front, he was a big man, hard and scarred, with thick sideburns and ruddy round cheeks. His reddish-colored hair was long in the back and curled over his shirt collar. With the duster unbuttoned, Will could see his gun belt heavily studded with bullets, his Colt slung low and tied to his leg. A gun-for-hire like Zach Marlowe, Will surmised that it was Ike Devlin who had ambushed him from behind at the saloon.

"I...I've got Roy outside," he said. "I brought him home."

"Is he drunk again?" Sam Granger asked in disgust.

"No, sir. No, Mr. Granger. He's dead, too," Ike Devlin told him.

The room was still. Sam Granger said nothing. He did not move at all and his face did not betray any emotion. With steady expression, he looked at Ike Devlin the same as if he had said, "There's a full moon out tonight."

"Fool boy," Granger muttered. "What happened?" he finally asked.

"He was shot in Enterprise. At Spanish Red's. Killed by this man here."

Granger looked at Will with narrow eyes. He recognized him as the farmer in the sheriff's office.

"And he's still alive? Why didn't you kill him? You're paid to take care of Grangers."

Granger slapped Ike Devlin across the right cheek, making a loud cracking sound in the quiet of the room.

"Thought you might want to take care of him yourself, sir," Devlin cautiously retorted, rubbing his cheek.

Sam Granger pondered and nodded. "You're right. I do." Then he looked at Will. "Tell me why: why did you kill my boy?"

"He drew down on me. Your business associate Marlowe, too. I had no choice, they were trying to kill me." Will paused and then acknowledged—more to himself than to Granger, "Even if they hadn't, I might still have killed them."

Will had no expectation of remaining alive much longer, so why go to his grave with a lie on his lips? Having faced death a number of times, he was not afraid, just disappointed. Disappointed in himself. Disappointed that he would not live to see certain things.

"Why would he draw down on you?" Sam Granger asked. "Was it because of that altercation with the Indian?"

"Because," Will said, "he and Marlowe murdered Sheriff Caulder. There were witnesses. They ambushed him, the pair of them with a couple of your other hired guns. Sneaked up on him in the dark. Your son was rotten to the core. I know there's no law on the Pecos anymore, except yours. But tonight, there was mine. I was going to put them in jail to wait for the circuit judge to come through."

"It was the sheriff's own fault," said Granger. "He couldn't be bought or bullied. And he didn't know when to leave well-enough alone."

Will bristled. He realized that Noble Caulder's death was part of Sam Granger's plan. He tried to break free of the two regulators on either side of him. Ike Devlin grabbed him and hit Will in the face with the back of his hand, and then doubled his huge fist and punched him hard in the stomach. Sam Granger held a hand up to him. He rose from his high-backed chair, removed his glasses, laid them on the desk and in two great strides confronted Will.

"Before I kill you," he said, quietly and coldly, squaring up his shoulders, "I want to know two things: how did a farmer like you get the drop on a professional gunman like Marlowe, and why do you care about the law here? No one has troubled you. I haven't harmed you or interfered with your life in any way. All I wanted was to bring the railroad in and ship my beef. What skin is it off your nose if the railroad comes through Enterprise?" There was no suggestion of sadness or loss in his demeanor.

Will was puzzled by the man's reaction to the death of his son, as if he really hadn't comprehended Devlin's words. He looked the elder Granger in the face. "The railroad makes no difference to me either way. But it does matter to me how my neighbors and fellow citizens are treated. And it matters to me that your son murdered the best friend I ever had—a good, decent, man of character who was a hundred times the man your son would ever be—who didn't deserve to be shot down in cold blood."

"Well," Sam Granger said, his face hard-cast and his eyes smoldering. "You're about to join him." He brought his fist up holding a heavy silver revolver and pointed the barrel toward Will. He slowly pulled back the hammer and pulled the trigger. *Click!* The hammer fell on an empty chamber, and Granger broke into a grand laugh. The regulators looked at each other and nervously joined in the laughter.

Without warning, Granger raised his hand and with the butt of the gun knocked Will hard on the side of the head. Will reeled, but did not go down. Granger hit him again, and this time Will dropped to one knee.

"Get rid of him, and make sure his body isn't found," Granger ordered Devlin in a heavy, even tone. "But don't kill him too quick. As I'll be suffering, I want him suffering too. Long and painful." He paused and added, "Give him to the *Llano Estacado*."

Spanish for 'Staked Plain,' the *Llano* was a white-hot desert kiln that covered endless leagues of barren table-land. It lay like a lesion south of Seminole and west of Sweetwater, between the Pecos River and the upper Brazos.

Now, again, Will was bundled over a saddle with his hands still tied behind him. The regulators were heavily armed and rode fresh horses. The five of them moved stealthily without rest for what remained of the moonlit night. Will could not tell how long that was. Riding fast, it seemed a number of hours went by.

Bouncing along and listening to the pounding of the horses' hooves, Will pictured Beth and Billy. He remembered things they had done together and places they had gone—on picnics, swimming in the river, or rocking gently on the porch swing during cool autumn nights. He pictured his farm and thought of riding his beautiful appaloosa, Bedford; he remembered his wedding night; he recalled the day his son was born and every small event that had occurred during the course of it.

He hoped his family would not grieve for him for too long. He hoped Beth would find a new husband, a kind person who would love and care for her the way she deserved. He hoped his son would grow to be a man of honor and of courage and that he would make something of his life. Most of all, Will hoped his family would remember him across the years.

There was little talk among the *pistoleros*. Leading the way, Ike Devlin rode fifty yards ahead of the three others. When they finally drew rein, day was breaking. The moon went down as the dawn came up and, watching from the horse's flank, Will could see shafts of red light burning just above the eastern horizon.

Devlin was the first to dismount. He removed the coiled rope from his saddle and went over to Will. "End of the line, farmer," he said.

Yanking Will off the horse, Devlin tied him underneath his arms and across his chest, cinching the knot tight. He instructed two other regulators to remove Will's boots. Paying out rope,

Devlin went back to his mount, tied and knotted the end of the rope around his saddle horn. Then he swung up onto the big roan.

"Time for a ride," Devlin said. "Compliments of Mr. Granger."

"Hurry, Ike," one regulator said. "We need to get out of here pretty quick. Day's coming fast and we're in Dagger Flats. On the edge of the Comancheria."

A broad section of the *Llano Estacado*, the Comancheria, was a no-man's land full of high plateaus and mesas and ravines. The terrain was ideally suited to Indian-style warfare and ambushes from horseback, at which the Comanche excelled. It was home to roving bands of fierce, heavily armed war parties. Even the Army dreaded to come here, despite its superiority in numbers and firepower. Every soldier's worst nightmare was to ride into the Comancheria and be taken prisoner.

"Don't worry," Devlin said. "We'll be gone in plenty of time." He dug his spurs into his horse and commenced with a powerful jerk, pulling Will along.

At first, Will ran behind him, stumbling but remaining on his feet. But then Devlin began to ride faster. Will could not keep up. Hands still tied behind his back, he tripped and fell on his stomach. Devlin dragged him along on his belly, drawing him between joint-mesquite trees with their sharp-pointed thorns, through clusters of mescal bean and sage plants; bristling prickly pear, *yucca* and *choya* cactus; and dense thickets of bee-shrub, ripping and shredding his clothing—the finery that he had worn to the Bransom's anniversary party—and flaying his skin into bloody strips. The pain was mind-numbing; like being continually scalded with boiling water.

Devlin relentlessly spurred his horse, pulling Will along a bed of jagged rock and cactus. They disappeared behind a grove of mesquite, coming in sight again through a stand of prickly pear. He rode figure-eight's, ramming Will head-first into the sharp spines and spires before dragging him back to the other regulators, where he finally reined to a halt and checked his mount. Nearly unconscious, Will rolled on to his side and tried getting to his feet. But his legs gave out and he crumpled back to the ground.

Sitting high atop his horse, one *pistolero* laughed. "Thirsty?" he said. "Here, take a drink." He lifted his canteen, unscrewed the cap and poured a trickle of water out on the ground. "Go ahead, drink. Lick it off the sand."

"Let's kill him now, Ike," another said. "And get out of here. This place gives me the spooks." He took out his pistol.

"Put the gun away, Clell," Ike Devlin told him. "You heard the boss. That's too quick. We leave him here to suffer like Mr. Granger said. He's half-past dead anyway. We'll let the *Llano* finish him. And besides, we don't want to draw attention with a gunshot. Turkey-buzzards got to wait for their meal. But it's getting hot. They won't have to wait too long."

"*Vaya con Dios, compadre*," the man named Clell said to Will. He laughed.

"Let's ride," Ike Devlin said. "We'll make for that water hole we passed. Rest and water the horses away from the Comancheria."

From his back, Will watched them trot off. He heard coyotes howling nearby, but he had no strength to move. Then he closed his eyes.

When he opened them, the sun was high in the sky. His skin felt on fire and was covered in dried blood. He sat up painfully and glanced around. There was no shade, no cloud, no shelter from the sun, anywhere that he could see. Nightfall would be a long time coming. As he struggled to stand, he decided to look for a cave or an outcrop; anywhere he could hide from the pitiless sun. He twisted and wiggled his wrists to increase circulation. His fingers were going numb again. He started to walk slowly and unsteadily through the desolation of sand and rock, in what he judged to be a northerly direction. The ground to his bare feet was like a bed of glowing coals. The heat was smothering him.

Without shade or water, he did not think he would last out the day.

Hours passed. The flame of the sun gripped him like jaws of a vise. He staggered along across the parched plain, heat waves shimmering, up burnt hillocks and across dry gulches, stopping to rest more and more frequently. Alone and exhausted, skin blistered and lips cracked, his tongue swollen from thirst, he felt reality slipping from him. He looked hopefully for any sign of the Comanches. He prayed that they would come soon and emancipate him from his mad march to nowhere, killing him quickly so he could finally sleep.

His thoughts and emotions fluctuated like the waves of heat beating on his broken body. He tried striking a bargain with God or with the devil, at this point he did not care which: *Lord or Lucifer,* he thought, *let me escape this curse of a desert and I'll do your work forever, good or evil. So I can hunt down Sam Granger and his gunmen and send them to you. Grant me this one thing and nothing else. Then take my soul or destroy it, I'll hand it over gladly.*

He staggered on until even his taste for vengeance could no longer support him. Overhead, he saw buzzards circling, dipping and rising, knowing he was dying. He thought of Beth and Billy again, and the last look of disappointment that his son gave him. And he thought of Noble. He longed to turn back time so this day had never happened. Finally he collapsed.

Will fell into a dream. From the vast darkness of the desert floor, he was being lifted by many hands. Water—cool, clear, life-giving water—flowed over his face and into his mouth, across his chest and arms. Was he seeing through God's eyes? Was he between earth and heaven?

The wasteland began to lighten with the soaring moon. Serene stars came out, and wheeled across the limitless sky. Then he was riding a tall horse with no saddle. But he could neither grip the reins nor sit the animal properly; he kept slumping over.

On either side a horseman held him upright to keep him from falling.

Up ahead was a column of riders cantering single file on unshod hooves, occasionally becoming lost from view in the intervening darkness. He made out jagged outlines of cliff-rock. He heard soft voices all around speaking in a language he did not understand.

Then he felt himself being lifted again. Strong hands set him down on a bed of soft cedar boughs draped with a blanket of buffalo leather. The face of a beautiful Indian woman hovered close to his. Gently, she wiped his face and his body all the way down to his burned feet. With deft fingers she massaged fragrant, soothing oil into his torn, broken skin.

Beginning to awaken, he tried to sit up, but could not. The woman was still there, on her knees, kneading him, rubbing him. Will wanted desperately to speak to her, to thank her and to question her, but could find no voice. A tall man with long hair, burnt gold by the sun, suddenly appeared over the woman and eased Will back down by his shoulders.

"Do not be afraid," the man said. "You are safe. Rest now. We talk later."

The man was dark-eyed and dark-skinned, with a hawk nose and high cheekbones. He wore knee-length moccasins, buckskin britches and a leather vest with no shirt.

"Who... are you?" Will managed to croak. He was beginning to realize this was no dream.

"I am *Pea'hochso*," the man said. "In English it means 'Big Eagle.' You are in my tipi."

The Comanche said something to the woman in the strange tongue. And then he was gone.

Will closed his eyes. His mind whirled in darkness. Then he slept.

Chapter Six

In the stillness of the tipi, William Hart dreamed of a time long past. A small cottage in Mississippi, a girl he had loved and lost, a friend named Noble Caulder. A cruel and unforgiving war, and many close brushes with death. He had always figured it was only a matter of time before his luck ran out.

Miraculously, he had managed to survive more than three years of war galloping along behind General Nathan Bedford Forrest—known by many as the "wizard of the saddle." The cavalry of the Army of Tennessee, operating across five states, had fought and beaten what seemed like a million well-armed Union troops. But time and numbers were not on Will Hart's side.

Over in Virginia, Jeb Stuart and his boys were getting all the publicity. Here, in the Department of the West, General Forrest was getting all the victories. Yet no matter how many Yankees they killed, there were always more to take their place. Will did not know any statistics, but three years of staying alive while riding point in a partisan brigade seemed like living on borrowed time.

The commander himself was a marked man. Fearless to the point of insanity, Nathan Bedford Forrest loved nothing better than raising a saber to his enemies. After Stonewall Jackson, dead now a year, he was the Confederate general most feared by the Union troops. There was a bounty on his head. But he had more lives than an Egyptian cat. His men believed that no Yankee ever spawned could match his generalship, let alone slay him—that included Sherman and Sheridan and Grant. The men were right: Nathan Bedford Forrest rode where he liked and struck where he wanted. He knew no limit of cunning or brave steel. He scourged the country like a Cossack and no Union bivouac felt safe at night if he was within a hundred miles.

Now his partisan rangers, nearly three-thousand of them, were back from Tennessee and back in Mississippi. The weather this June morning was hot and humid, with a rising mist, after the heavy rains of the previous night. The gray horsemen were moving east, from Tupelo, on their way to intercept a nine-thousand man Union force headed to destroy General Forrest's main supply bases: the Mobile & Ohio railroad depots at Tupelo and Corinth.

This particular morning—a bit past ten o'clock—William Thomas Hart, Captain of Cavalry, C.S.A., was on point for Company N, Colonel Noble Caulder's unit, Mississippi volunteers out of Adams County. They were seasoned raiders, experienced in irregular warfare. Though outnumbered three to one, the Confederates were anticipating a victory today. Their general's genius, they knew, would more than compensate for their inferior numbers.

Approaching the hamlet of Brice's Crossroads and the narrow wooden bridge over Tishomingo Creek, Will checked his horse, a four-year-old roan-colored gelding he had named Jeff Davis, when he saw two gray riders in the distance. He thought they might be part of a returning patrol. He put up his field glasses, and turned the eyepieces around until the riders came clear into focus. The scene was of his two commanding officers side by side. He spurred his horse forward to greet them, snapping off a salute as he drew rein.

"General Forrest, Colonel Caulder," he said.

"Captain Hart," Nathan Bedford Forrest said, casually returning Will's salute with his gloved right hand. "Which units are closest behind you?"

"Two brigades, sir," Will told him. "Colonel Caulder's and Colonel Rucker's. Seven-hundred fifty men. Our lead elements."

"I want them formed at once for battle," Forrest said to Noble Caulder.

"Yes, Sir," the Colonel said. "But should we wait for the rest of the army and the artillery to catch up? They shouldn't be far back. Right, Captain?"

"A mile back, maybe. No more," said the young officer.

"We could hit them with our full strength," Noble Caulder said.

"A good plan, Colonel," Forrest said. "But hold them back until I give the order. I'll bait the Federals into thinking our attack force is small. When they come rushing forward to crush it, half-exhausted, we'll bury them under an avalanche of lead." He turned to Will and said, "The Colonel and I have just scouted the road leading to the causeway. The Tishomingo is overflowing from the rain. The road crosses a plateau of soggy bottomland. It's narrow and shin-deep with mud. We'll strike them in the flank along their route of march, while they're slogging, all bunched up; then hammer them with canister fire and send in our main body. We'll annihilate the whole force. Form both brigades immediately." He smiled slightly and his eyes gleamed at the thought of the carnage he would inflict.

General Forrest lived to fight Yankees. Six feet, two inches tall and two-hundred pounds, with shoulder-length black hair, a Van Dyke beard and piercing black eyes, Forrest looked the way Will thought a man of war should look. His gray hat, brim upturned on one side, carried the Stars and Bars and had a gold-tasseled cord around it; his tunic sported Major-General's stars on each side of the collar. The uniform was brown with wear and saddle-stained, like Will's; his boots were made of fine leather but covered with mud, also like Will's.

The General spun his mount and rode toward the Confederate column, leaving Will alone with his Colonel.

"Get up to the bridge, Will," Noble said. "I'll send you a courier. I'm going back to unlimber the guns and double-time both brigades. When they get here, take up angled positions in the woods on both sides of the creek."

"Yes, Sir," Will said. He kicked his heels into his horse and rode back to the bridge.

When he got there, the sun was burning away the mist. Oppressively humid, the heat was building rapidly. The low hum of insects pervaded the air and buzzed about his face. The afternoon would be a boiling cauldron—"Rebel weather," as the Northern troops called it. Will took the heat as a good omen.

The horse's iron-shod hooves clopped across the wooden bridge. Will stopped at the far end and, putting up the field glasses, swept the terrain. There was no sign of any Yankees. He turned Jeff Davis into the woods, near a tangle-brushed hillock where he could watch the road, and dismounted, waiting for the courier. He took a green apple from his saddle bag and held it up. The horse looked a moment at his master, then ate it quickly and licked Will's hand.

"You're a good horse," Will said. "I'm sorry to have to put you through this, boy." He patted its neck and stroked its withers. The horse whinnied ever so softly and rubbed his nose against Will's gray sleeve. "Do you know who I named you for? The President of the Confederate States of America, that's who. But he wasn't always President. No. Not when I met him."

Will reminisced that day in 1857, some seven years earlier, when Senator Jefferson Davis himself came to visit at his family's home. It was the proudest moment of Will's life. The Senator, one of the most prominent politicians in the country, who had been Secretary of War during President Pierce's administration, had traveled halfway across Mississippi to meet him, all the way from his Brierfield plantation to Natchez. It was the Senator's policy to personally meet any young Mississippian he sponsored for entry into the United States Military Academy at West Point.

Everyone in Natchez had buzzed over the news of his visit. Everyone, that is, except Will's father, Jackson Hart. "Well, that boy'll be putting on airs now, like he's better than everybody. I know this is going to end up costing me something," was all he could manage to grunt when Will's mother, Sarah Hart, had told him about it.

Neither Will nor his mother had any idea where the old man hid that day. Drinking himself into a stupor in some saloon, Will thought. Or sleeping off a drunk at the livery in town. It was best that Senator Davis not see him. That way Jackson Hart could not embarrass them.

Jackson Hart was selfish, mean-tempered and hard-drinking. When Will was young, he was afraid of his father. Now that he was older, Will despised him, and saw him as nothing more than a coward and a bully. Will wished things had been different. He wished for a father who he could respect and who would show him love. He wished for a father who would treat his mother with the affection and dignity she deserved. And now, he wished for a father that he could share this moment of triumph with.

Jefferson Davis, nearing fifty years, came dressed in a black frock coat, white ruffled shirt, and wide black bow tie. He was tall and erect, of military bearing. He was nearly blind in his left eye; it was glazed and out of focus. His long hair was dark and he had an angular jaw and high cheekbones, like an Indian's. A graduate of West Point, class of 1828, and a hero of the Mexican War, he was one of the leading lights in the marbled halls of the United States Senate and a major spokesman for the Southern point of view in Congress.

The three had tea and buttermilk pie together that afternoon, after which Sarah Hart, having fussed and hovered long enough over Davis, thanked the Senator profusely and retired to the other room so her son could be alone with him.

"Senator Davis," young Will Hart had said, sitting beside him at the dining room table. "This is such a great honor for my mother and me. I don't know how to begin thanking you. For you to send me to West Point—for me to actually meet you— well, it's unimaginable."

The Senator crossed his legs and smiled. "The honor is mine," Jefferson Davis told him, his eyes twinkling as he spoke. "You are a true son of Mississippi. You have made excellent grades. You're a fine horseman. And you are a mature and serious young man of good character. Your teachers—they have written to me personally—think very highly of you. As you know, we are in a crisis of Union. Our country and our army will desperately need men like you: sober, intelligent, and upright, in the coming months and years. Knowing something of the Military Academy, I can say with confidence that West Point will be the better for your going."

Will felt proud and full of emotion. "Mr. Davis, sir…Senator Davis… Secretary, sir…I…I won't let you down. I promise," he managed to choke.

Jefferson Davis smiled again. "I believe you. But don't fret. I was near the bottom of my West Point class. I don't think I have done too badly. Unless you should ask the republicans. But always remember: certain Northerners will take any opportunity to demolish a Mississippian. Give them no fodder. The eyes of our state are upon you. I know you will make us proud. If there is ever anything I can do to help, you have only to ask."

Will graduated in 1861, fortieth in a class of seventy-nine. But, as one professor told him, while he would never be one of the great military intellectuals, he was a born tactician. First at West Point in infantry and cavalry tactics, he became a master at the use of small arms. He had always been a crack shot. The only classmate who could rival him was George Armstrong Custer, now fighting on the Yankee side. But Will was an even better shot. If he hadn't been such a free-wheeling officer, inclined to overrule orders and issue his own, he might've become a general by now.

The images of meeting Jefferson Davis vanished when Will heard the clip-clop of the approaching horseman. It was Sergeant McShane. His ragged butternut uniform was dirty, as was his gray kepi. Just as he arrived, Will heard a rumbling in the distance. Leaving Jeff Davis in the brush, he stepped out onto the edge of the bridge and motioned McShane over. Listening, he put up the field glasses and quickly surveyed the land before him. He could not see any movement.

"Orders, sir?" McShane said without dismounting.

Will held up his right hand, signaling the sergeant to keep silent. He lowered the glasses and said, "Ride back and tell Colonel Caulder that the Federal cavalry will be here within the hour. Their artillery and caissons will be right behind. Tell him to get both brigades up here fast."

McShane turned his mount and sped back toward the gray column.

When the men—dismounted cavalry—started arriving, Will positioned them in the woods on either side of Tishomingo Creek to cover the muddy plateau in front. Musket fire erupted as soon as the Union horsemen came out of the timber, a half-mile from the bridge. The throng of blue began plodding their way through the thick mud. A volley of Confederate bullets flew into and around them. A score of men fell at once. The Union soldiers fired back in the direction of the smoke.

Resting his Robinson .52 carbine in the crotch of an oak tree, Will put his front sight on the chest of a blue officer, a horseman with an upraised saber. He squeezed off a shot, smelling smoke in the dank air; the rifle's report rang in his ears.

The Union Major came out of his saddle and fell into the mud. Will cursed the cruelty of war and the wasted lives. The cavalry around him shouted and fired their Spencer rifles wildly in all directions. Both Confederate brigades in the brush poured out a heavy enfilading fire, thundering like echoes across the battlefield. Raking the lines, it was as if the Union troops had hit a trip wire. Every gray musket-barrel flashed yellow and belched soot-colored smoke. Scrambling for cover, the soldiers in blue fanned out and attempted to move forward and counterattack.

From somewhere a bugle pealed, and Will saw the Union infantry storm out of the trees and begin trudging onto the muddy field in support of the cavalry, just as General Forrest had expected. Some were already collapsing from heat exhaustion. Small units, clusters of riflemen, began to penetrate the woods in an effort to clear the graybacks. More dense masses of blue troops pressed on with hollow screams of war and a crackling of armament, in ever greater numbers. The fighting in the thickets grew furious; in some places troops fought to the death with revolvers and sawed-off shotguns at point-blank range, some with swords and bayonets, some disparately swung empty rifles, using the stocks as clubs.

Overhead, Will heard the roar of cannons and shells whistling at random. The ground shook as General Forrest's artillery began hammering the Union troops, pounding the plateau and the timberline with canister and grapeshot. Union batteries took up a vicious counter-fire and the woods around Will groaned and smoked under the bombardment. And then, without warning, there was a lull.

It lasted only long enough for Nathan Bedford Forrest, now on the field with the main body of his army, to launch a full-scale assault. He was in his shirtsleeves because of the heat, on his big sorrel horse, his gray coat hanging from his saddle horn. Saber in hand, General Forrest rode among his officers, issuing orders and checking his line from atop his mount. Trotting up onto the bridge, he commanded his forward elements to attack the enemy full-bore at the sound of the bugles, and with triumphal swiftness led them in a charge.

"Get up, men," the General challenged. "Every man must charge the Federals and give them agony. We're going to destroy every last one of those blue bellies. One gray is worth fifty blues. Forward, men! For the Confederacy!"

The bugles sounded. Will swung up onto Jeff Davis and led two dozen horsemen from Company N along the banks of the creek. Thundering toward the heaving blue mass, he drew one of his two big Colt revolvers. He fired three shots; three Union cavalry pitched from their horses by the dead-center force of his lead bullets; the rest turned and galloped back toward the trees. Will and his men fired madly at the fleeing targets, then took aim at the infantry running wildly among the trees and through the brush. A number of Union soldiers jumped into the creek to escape the fight and began swimming downstream, the water tinged in red. Others threw down their weapons and tried to surrender. In places, Union small arms blazed back at the onrushing gray cavalry with lethal accuracy.

Riding hard and firing through a curtain of thick smoke, his eyes watering, Will could hear the screaming of wounded men and beasts across the length of the battlefield. A bullet shrieked past Will's face and struck a comrade behind him. Artillery shells continued whistling in. The noise was deafening; the field was seething with smoke and death. One after another, shells began bursting directly in front of the charging Confederates, almost on top of them. Horses and mules with gaping wounds lay mangled and kicking in Will's path, bellowing hoarsely. Corpses of soldiers began piling up, mostly blue, but with some gray thrown in. Will emptied both Colts, reloaded, and kept shooting.

Then, for no reason that Will could see, Jeff Davis began slowing down. Will gave him both heels but he slowed and slowed until he was trotting and then skipping and then walking, unsteadily. Then he swayed on his hind legs, wobbled, and buckled over onto his right side.

As the gelding toppled, Will kicked out of the stirrups to avoid being pinned beneath the dying horse and dove out onto his shoulder and side, rolling four or five feet into the wet brush. Losing his grip on both handguns, he struggled to his feet and saw some Union infantry bearing down on him. Oddly, the first thing he noticed was their stripes—there was a corporal, a sergeant and two privates.

He hoped they meant to take him prisoner. As an officer, he might have value to them. But then he saw it was not so. All four troopers were snarling and pointing their guns.

Through a medley of smoke and fire, he stood waiting for the bullets to strike him. The thought of his bride, Abby, flashed in his mind. He had not seen her in more than a year. Since their marriage in 1862, they had spent a grand total of two months together. Now he would never see Abby again. He would die in these forbidden woods without the chance to say goodbye or to tell her how much he loved her one last time. Covered with dust and smoke and the sweat of battle, Will raised his hands high above his head, still hoping.

But the enemy was not buying it. "We don't take no Johnnies prisoner," one yelled. "We kill 'em." He cocked his pistol and took dead aim.

Then a shot rang out; the Union soldier fell forward onto his face. Then three more shots, in quick succession, dropped the others. A gray blur came sweeping up, leaned from the saddle, reached down, and grasped Will by the forearm.

It was the strong grasp of Colonel Noble Caulder, a grasp signifying a friendship and a bond that would last a life time.

"C'mon, Will!" he screamed, pulling Will up and behind him. He kicked his spurs in hard and the big cavalry horse dashed away, clattering and bouncing madly through the brush back in the direction of the gray lines. Union bullets whizzed past them, slicing through leaves and plinking off trees.

"Blue bellies!" Noble yelled back over his shoulder through a bank of smoke. "You missed!"

Both men laughed hysterically in relief. In this terrifying and thrilling panorama of war, they had outwitted the blue troops, again. Outwitted them, yes, but could never really defeat them. There were just too many.

Memories of a thousand other fights and skirmishes came over Will all at once. He jerked, and briefly woke himself from the feverish slumber. He tried to turn his head, but he couldn't move. He tried to speak, but no sound came past his parched throat and dry lips. Through blurred eyes, he could only see the dimly lit dome of the buffalo-hide tipi, and the kind face of the Comanche woman. He closed his eyes again.

Through a fog of gray and blue and a veil of red blood, he could still hear the hysterical laughter ringing in his ears, as if it was someone else's laughter that had welled up from across the years.

By 1865, however, Will Hart was not laughing. There was nothing left for him when he went home at war's end. Will's heart sank when he learned that Abby was dead. At twenty-two, of fever. His mother, Sarah Hart, was also dead, and no one knew what had become of Jackson Hart or if he was even alive. Noble Caulder had left Mississippi and lit out for Texas, where he had become a lawman. The state had been devastated. Natchez was under Union occupation and martial law. The Southern people were a conquered enemy.

One year after the surrender, a letter arrived for Will. It was from Noble Caulder. He was marshalling, he said, and his town needed another, a good gun; the place was wild and lawless, practically a war zone. The pay was thirty a month plus room and board. Because there weren't exactly a host of applicants, any ex-Confederates willing to take the job could have their citizenship restored at once by the Federal administration. Would Will be interested?

He was interested. Quickly he put his affairs in order, saddled a horse, collected his guns, put fresh flowers on Abby's grave, and hung a sign on the front door: SOLD, GONE TO TEXAS. Westward bound, Will Hart headed for the border town of El Paso.

"Do you swear," he could hear Marshal Noble Caulder saying, "to uphold and enforce the laws of the United States of America and the State of Texas?"

The afternoon was hot and sunny. Will and Noble were standing in the adobe-brick marshal's office in El Paso. Through the window, Will could see his horse, Stonewall, out at the tie rail on main street, shaking off flies.

"I swear," Will replied, his right hand raised and looking his friend square in the eye.

Noble pinned the badge engraved with *Deputy, U.S. Marshal* on Will's shirt. "This piece of silver will have your word in it. Your word to me and your word to yourself. That's all that counts."

"Have I ever broken it?"

"Never. And it's too late to start now. For either of us."

They shook hands and Noble clapped him on the shoulder.

Noble sat down on a big brown chair of cracked leather stuffed with horse hair. He propped his feet up on the desk, and sipped lemonade from a beer mug. Will sat on the desk with his back against the wall, drinking cold coffee from a tin cup. He was wearing range clothes and a black slouch hat. He carried a long-barreled Walker .44 on his leg and a Colt .45 Peacemaker in a side holster. Both had walnut grips and oversized hammers and triggers. The initials W.H. were cut over the trigger guards.

"From what you've said, we've got a lot of work," Will told him. "When do I meet the other deputies?"

"You don't. There aren't any."

"What do mean, there aren't any? How can there not be any deputies in a devil's hole like this? You'd need six at least."

"You and I are it," Noble said. "They couldn't find anybody else dumb enough to come to work here." He grinned, laughed and slapped his thigh.

Will looked at him and scowled, but not for long. Noble was grinning from ear to ear and Will could not keep from laughing as well. "Heaven help me," he said. "I'm in the hands of a lunatic."

For two years they worked to bring order to the southwest. El Paso had become a sanctuary for stage robbers, cattle rustlers, horse thieves, card sharks, bank robbers, army deserters, claim jumpers, renegades and desperados. Three U.S. Marshals had been murdered before Noble Caulder's arrival and two others had just disappeared; the people of the town had locked their doors and hid themselves at sundown.

Every day Noble and Will broke up fist, knife and gun fights, laying their lives on the line, battling the worst killers and thugs on the frontier. They arrested so many troublemakers that the jail could not hold them. They had to send to Fort Stockton for prison wagons to serve as free-standing cells. At times, they were forced to hunt and gun down the worst of the worst, without trial and without fanfare.

No matter how much death Will had seen or inflicted, he had never made his peace with it. The taking of life, any life, even a worthless one like the cut-throats and gunslingers around El Paso, was a dreadful thing.

Word of the duo's successes had spread throughout the state, and it wasn't long until Noble Caulder was asked to be the sheriff in the West Texas town of Enterprise, due south in Pecos County. Noble accepted the job, confessing his longing for peaceful, quieter times, and turned his Marshal's badge over to Will Hart.

More scenes from his past came to Will and unfolded in front of him as he tossed and turned in the quiet of the darkened tipi. Will suddenly saw an old acquaintance, Cole Younger, come into the tipi. He took off his hat, looked down and smiled. Belle, his woman, was with him, her arm around his waist. Then they were gone and Will was sitting in the Longhorn saloon playing poker and meeting Cole for the first time.

He heard the piano in the background and the laughter of pretty girls, saw the long bar and the big mirror and the whiskey bottles and the kegs. He smelled the beer and watched a dark-haired girl in a long dress move up the stairs on the arm of a male companion; he saw the faces of the other players seated at the table.

There were four of them in the game: Will; a freckle-headed ranch hand they called Rusty from out near the salt flats; a gaunt-faced gambler in a white coat and stovepipe hat named Forbes; and a stranger in a tan slouch hat, with a sweeping mustache and dark circles under his eyes. His face was tawny brown from the sun and he wore high boots with the pants tucked in and carried a long-barreled Colt and a bowie knife in his belt. He had stopped in for a beer and asked if he could join the game.

Samantha Blue, one of the Longhorn girls, was standing behind Will. She had big blue eyes, which gave her the nickname, and hair the color of corn. She had on a turquoise dress with a tight bodice. Both her hands were on Will's shoulders.

"You've got a secret weapon, eh Marshal?" the stranger said as Will laid down a spade flush and raked in a pot. "You get that girl there to distract us. Then beat our brains out." He smiled pleasantly.

Will smiled back. "Just luck. I'm not that good of a poker player, although I enjoy the game. Your accent's familiar. Where are you from?"

"Missouri. Yours too. I know it ain't Texan."

"No. Mississippi," replied Will. There was something about this stranger Will liked.

"Where bouts?"

"Natchez. Grew up along the Trace. You?"

"Little farm in Harrisonville, below Joplin. Makes us practically neighbors. Who were you with in the war?"

"General Forrest."

The stranger nodded. "The best." He raised his beer mug. "To Nathan Bedford Forrest." Everyone at the table raised their glasses.

"To the General," Will said. "What about you?"

"Captain Quantrill."

"To Captain William Quantrill," Will said, clinking mugs with the stranger.

Will reached across the table to shake hands. About thirty years old, the man had a good solid grip. "The name's Will. Will Hart."

"Cole Younger," the stranger said. "I heard about you. You and another marshal, named Caulder. Word is anybody coming to these parts had better watch their step. Or they might not live long."

"Are we," Forbes, the gambler, said sourly, "going to play poker or gossip like women all day?" He was losing heavily.

"Don't you like women?" Samantha Blue asked him, leaning forward to catch his eye.

"We'll do both," Will said. "Go ahead, deal. Nobody's stopping you."

Snapping the cards loudly and glaring at Samantha Blue, Forbes dealt a new hand.

"I've heard your name too, Cole," Will said, picking up his cards and arranging them. They were playing five-card draw. "Didn't you and your kin ride with the James brothers? Robbed a Yankee railroad and bank once or twice, the way I heard it. What brings you so far from home?" He had taken a liking to Cole Younger.

"A woman. Name of Belle."

Will clucked his tongue and shook his head back and forth. "That's a name to remember. She must be one fine woman to ride a thousand miles for."

"Dad-blamedest woman I ever met."

"She yours?"

"Nope."

"Where is she now?"

Cole shook his head, sadly. "Married."

"Sorry about that."

"Yeah, me too."

"What are you doing in El Paso," Will queried. "Hope you haven't come to town with your belly full of bad intentions."

"No, Marshal. Not at all. I'm just passing through, on my way back to Missouri. I'm not looking for any trouble."

"Good. Keep it that way, while you're here."

"Oh, I will, Marshal."

The cowhand, Rusty, dropped a bill into the pot. "Bet one," he drawled.

Everybody called. Rusty held three jacks, which won. The gambler in the white coat threw his cards down in disgust. He had lost with two-pair, aces up. He scooped up the money he had left and stuffed it in his pocket. "I'm out. It's an outrage to lose to amateurs like you," he said and stalked off.

The poker game continued. Another stranger came into the Longhorn saloon. Slight of stature and cocky in manner, he was dressed in trail clothes with chaps, and he had long, greasy dark hair and a scraggly beard. His eyes were small and close together. He carried two nickel-plated revolvers in his belt. He went to the bar, ordered tequila and stood there, drinking and watching the game.

"Mind if I sit in?" he called across the barroom.

The cowboy looked at him and shrugged. "Come ahead. Long as your money is American."

"It is." He came over and sat in the chair Forbes had used.

They played for a while without conversation. The newcomer kept ordering tequila, betting wildly, and losing. When Cole Younger took three hands in a row, the stranger began accusing him.

"You're sandbagging me," he said to Cole. "You think I don't see the way you look at that marshal? Nobody's that lucky."

"That's the tequila talking," Cole Younger said. "Nobody's sandbagging anybody, Martin."

"You know me?"

"Yeah. I know who you are," said Cole.

"Then you know what I can do to you."

"Nobody," Will said, "is doing anything to anyone. Let's just play cards."

It was Will's deal. They played another hand. Cole won with a small straight over the new player's three kings.

"You sharks are all in it together!" he said. "It's a confidence trick. I'm getting my money back."

"That's wild talk," Will said. "You lost fair and square. So mind your mouth, and either play or leave the table."

"You think you're something because of that badge? You ain't nothing. You don't know who you're dealing with. Nobody cheats me, marshal or not. I've shot men for less."

"He's Clay Martin, marshal. *The* famous gunfighter," Cole Younger said with good-natured sarcasm. "They say he kills more than the typhus. Killed a man for snoring too loud, they say."

"They say, they say…" Clay Martin muttered, his voice trailing off as he threw back another tequila.

"I'm out. Done," Cole Younger said. He flipped his cards on the table, put his money in his pocket and started to get up.

"Oh, no you ain't," Martin said. Suddenly a silver revolver appeared in his hand. "You ain't out till I say you're out. You're staying until I get my money back."

"Put that pistol away," Will told him. "Before you get hurt."

Martin wheeled on him. "You challenging me, Marshal?"

"Sure," Will said. "I was thinking of a spelling bee."

Cole Younger laughed.

Embarrassed by the mockery, Clay Martin flushed red and cocked the hammer. He pointed the gun at Cole's head.

Before he could do anything else, Will stretched his leg out under the table, hooked his foot under the bottom rung of Martin's chair, yanked it hard, and spilled him onto the floor. Martin fell sprawling on his back. Quick as a cat, Will was up with the Colt out. He kicked the gun from Martin's hand, leaned down and with the butt of the .45 cracked him across the temple. Will took away the second revolver, stuck it in his belt, and grabbed Martin by the shirt collar. He dragged him to the door like a sack of rubbish.

"Lemme go, lemme go!" Clay Martin yelled, trying to twist away.

Will lost hold of him, then regained his grip. "You just committed the crime of attempted murder," he said. "It should cost you about ten years. Think about that next time you're in a card game."

"Marshal, no, please!" Martin hollered. "Let me go; I'll get out of El Paso fast."

"Tell me why I should let you just go?" asked Will.

"I'll give you something big. Something real big is gonna happen here today. And soon. In an hour, maybe. Maybe less. *Bandoleros* are coming."

Will released him. "What do you know about these *bandoleros*?"

"Let me go?" bargained Martin.

"Depends if I believe you. You'd better not be lying, boy."

"I ain't." Rubbing the big welt on his head, Clay Martin slowly got to his feet. "I was across the border this morning. I was in a little Mexican watering hole south of Juarez. I was drinking pulque and I overheard a man they called Barbosa talking to some others about what he planned to do today in El Paso."

"Feliciano Barbosa? What did he look like?"

"Thin mustache, scar under one eye."

"That's him. What was a punk like you doing in Mexico?"

"Selling horses," said Martin.

"That you rustled, no doubt," said Will.

Clay Martin said nothing.

"What were they planning?" queried Will.

"They were making a plan for getting some quick money, it sounded like," replied Martin.

"What else?"

"That's all I know. He said they'd ride in and ride out fast before anybody knew. I swear it's the truth."

"Get out of town," Will told him. "Right now."

"Can I have my guns back?"

"No. Now, get."

Clay Martin picked up his hat and hurried off.

"Do you want me to hang around and give you a hand with these *bandoleros*?" Cole Younger asked.

"Thanks," Will said looking Cole in the eye, "but I'll be fine. All in a day's work. Thanks anyway, Cole."

"I'll stop by for a drink before I leave," said Cole, extending his hand to the marshal. Will grasped it and nodded.

Will went quickly to the marshal's office. He slid open the wide heavy desk drawer and placed Clay Martin's pistols inside. Then he chose two bone-handled Colt .45 Peacemaker revolvers from among the pistols that were there. He loaded the cylinders of both Colts and stuck one in the front of his waistband and one in the back. Will then walked over and stood in front of the gun rack. He removed a Winchester .44-40 carbine that had a sling strap and a Remington sawed off. Cracking the barrel of the shotgun, he slipped in two 12-gauge buckshot shells and put six more in his pockets. He then loaded the Winchester and slung it over his shoulder. When he was ready, he went outside and looked around.

The main street was dry and sandy; the air was hot. The street was relatively quiet, but Will noticed a few townsfolk lingering on the boardwalk in front of the general store. A couple of saddled horses were hitched to a railing and little further down by the livery stable was a canvas-covered wagon and team.

Walking in the shade, head swinging from side to side, Will started up the street toward the main part of town. With keen eyes and keen ears, he watched. As he met the citizens, he cautioned them to clear the street. Beyond the general store he encountered a couple of the town's children, Pedro and Maria Ortega, playing bare-toed in the cool sand of the shade. With a firm, but even voice, he told them to get along home quickly.

"Is there going to be trouble, *Señor* Marshal?" the ten-year-old Pedro asked eagerly. The little girl's face flashed richly brown, as she tried hiding behind her brother.

"There may be. Now go. Get your little sister home *pronto*," Will told the boy.

But the timing was not right. Will had gone about fifty paces when he heard the low roar of trampling hooves and saw the dust rise at the edge of town. One dozen riders wearing broad black sombreros, riding side by side in two's, were turning on to the main street. Passersby scattered and flew in all directions as the horsemen came on.

They drew rein in front of the Longhorn saloon, where five or six dismounted and went inside. The rest sat their horses and waited in front of the hitching post. Will double-timed toward the direction of the riders.

Just before Will reached the saloon, he saw the *bandoleros* come out. They were dragging three young ladies from the Longhorn, shaking and slapping them to quiet their screams. They began tossing them up onto the horses.

Stepping down from the boardwalk and out into the center of sun-baked street—it was five o'clock and Will heard the clock on the bell tower striking—he called out to the horsemen.

"Barbosa," he called, standing as straight as a soldier. "Feliciano Barbosa."

The riders all checked their mounts and looked at him.

Feliciano Barbosa, wearing a huge black sombrero and a serape thrown back over the shoulder of his gun hand, grinned. He wore high black boots, shiny with pointed toes, heeled with long-roweled spurs of Mexican silver. In front of him on his saddle he held a girl. She was crying and trembling. It was Samantha Blue.

"*Hola, Señor* Marshal," Barbosa said in derisive boldness. His teeth showed yellow. "Nice to see you again. I heard your *compadre* is no longer with you, and you walk the street alone."

"I thought you were smarter than to come back here, Barbosa," Will said.

"A man must make his living somehow, no?" Barbosa grinned and shrugged his shoulders.

"So now you're a kidnapper instead of a horse thief and murderer?" He shook his head. "You're moving even lower in the world. Let the girls go."

"Will, oh, Will!" Samantha Blue cried. "Please help us!"

"The girls are not for me," the *bandolero* told him. "They bring a fine price in Mexico. Especially for the *rubias*. The ones with light skin and light hair. This one, though, I think I keep." He kissed Samantha Blue with savage force on the mouth and laughed.

"Lower the women," Will said. He raised the stubby scattergun and pointed it at the *bandoleros*. Two of them complied, dropping a pair of Longhorn girls to the ground. They ran back to the saloon without looking back.

"Let her go, Barbosa," Will said. "She's not for you." He wanted to keep Barbosa talking, trying to keep him distracted, waiting for an opportunity to end this standoff.

"Why you want this one so much, eh?" Barbosa asked. "There are plenty of *gringas rubia.* Why you need this one?"

"Let her go and ride out," said Will. "Then I'll let all of you live today. But if you ever come back: *ai, mi madre!*" With his left hand he made the sign of the cross.

Barbosa tossed his head back and laughed loudly. "Ah, *Señor* Marshal. *Muy bueno.* Where do you like me to go?"

Will shrugged. "They say Chihuahua is nice this time of year."

"Kill him, *jefe,* and be done," a *bandolero* said, drawing a rifle from its saddle sheath. *"Vamanos."*

Barbosa tilted back his sombrero, exposing his greasy black hair that looked like a dead raven. His grin faded and his eyes turned to slits. "That's a lot of guns you're wearing, *gringo.* You must be expecting trouble."

"There's never trouble in my streets." With the sawed off hanging in his right hand, Will wrapped his finger around both triggers. "Trouble's all back yonder. In the cemetery."

"You think about sending me there? I have many *pistoleros*. You are one *gringo loco*. I think maybe I send you there. Then I come to El Paso any time at all."

"Let the girl go," said Will, continuing to size up the situation.

"If you try to shoot me with that," Barbosa said, "you only shoot the girl."

Will nodded and smiled. *"Sí.* You're right."

Without another word and with a whip of a hand, Barbosa drew his long-barreled six-shooter and fired in succession at Will. The marshal wheeled, the bullets narrowly missing him. Quick as lightning, Will threw up the shotgun and fired with both barrels, blasting the legs out from under Barbosa's horse. Blood spurted from the shattered limbs and tufts of horseflesh flew; the animal screamed and pitched forward, throwing Samantha Blue and Feliciano Barbosa six feet forward and into the middle of the dusty street.

"Go, Samantha, run!" Will shouted as he drew his Walker .44 and ducked, crouching low at the first crack of *bandolero* rifles.

As the girl dashed toward the Longhorn saloon, where the other two women had fled, Barbosa fired. Before Will could stop him, he nailed her in the back as she was about to go through the saloon doors. She staggered and fell hard, with a trembling hand outstretched, and then stiffened and lay motionless on her left side.

Will vaulted, diving head-long behind a water trough. A continuous fire-fight ensued. Bullets thudded into the wooden trough and whistled by. He rose to his knee and let loose with both sidearms.

Bandoleros began falling from their rearing horses. Guns were spitting lead at a murderous rate. In the smoke and confusion some attempted to gallop off; panicked, they could not control their frightened and whirling mounts. Several animals caught lead and tumbled, spilling the riders and creating a crazed, confused clutter all along the street.

He emptied the contents of the Walker .44 and then the Colt .45 Peacemaker and brought up both bone-handled Colts from his waistband. Bullets zipped. The *bandoleros* shot frantically in a dozen directions, shattering window glass and chipping adobe walls. Then all was quiet.

He could see the *bandoleros* on the ground, their mouths gaping, panting, screaming, their bodies writhing and wriggling like snakes; but he could not hear them. The gunfire had deafened him. Three more rounds were all he fired; there was no further need. There was nobody left alive to shoot.

Will stood up. His face was streaked dark with gunpowder and streaming with sweat; drops rolled off his chin. He swung the Winchester from side to side covering the dead men and animals lying on the ground.

Slowly, silently, the marshal walked the street, inspected the carnage, and took the tally: twelve *bandoleros*, four horses, one Longhorn woman, and…and…one six-year-old girl.

Will's heart sank. He walked over and saw the limp body of little Maria Ortega. She was lying face down on the boardwalk, shot through the chest, patches of dark red staining her homespun blue dress. An innocent angel caught in a satanic crossfire. Will grew deathly cold and felt deathly sick.

For Will, everything seemed to stop at that moment, to freeze in time. The only movement that appeared to continue was the slow-motion drip of red from men and horses, blood trickling, life ebbing away, again, in the El Paso dirt.

Will resigned as Marshal before the day was out. He vowed he would never again put on a gun or a badge.

Two weeks later he received a telegram from his friend Noble Caulder. "Come to the Pecos," the words said. "Fishing is good, land is cheap and folks are friendly. There's a preacher's daughter here I'd like you to meet. Her name is Elizabeth Cullen…"

A shaft of daylight and soft voices chased away the memories. Will stirred, and the present claimed him. The buffalo-hide flaps that covered the tipi entrance were thrown back and two gray figures ducked in. One was the long-haired Comanche who had spoken to him…when? Last night? Last week? The one who called himself Big Eagle. The other was an Indian Will had never seen before. He had two long braids and a bronze face that bore traces of paint or pigment.

Both men were armed, but somehow, Will did not think he was their prisoner. If they wanted, they could have left him for buzzard-bait in the *Llano Estacado*. He sat up stiffly and leaned on his elbows. He noticed that he had on buckskin britches.

"You talked much in your sleep," Big Eagle said. "Can you talk now, awake?"

"I can," Will said, registering that the Comanche spoke English well. His entire body ached and there was a ringing in his ears. But his mind was clearing. He was glad to be alive. He felt hungry and thirsty. "Thank you for saving my life. Why did you?"

"You have done great bravery, one against many. You might be useful. We have the same enemy. There is a saying," the Comanche told him. "The enemy of my enemy is my friend."

"Your enemy is Sam Granger?" Will asked.

"And the men he has brought here."

"Yes," Will said. "There are plenty more. They ride for him. He pays plenty for killers."

Big Eagle looked at Will. "I know."

"You know what happened at the saloon in Enterprise?" Will asked.

"I am war-chief of the Quahadi Comanche. We are at war. I must have many eyes and ears in many places to keep alive."

"It's not easy to keep alive during war," Will said. "I know that."

"No," Big Eagle said. "It is not easy for the Comanche to keep alive even during peace. But the life of a warrior belongs to his people. I will die gladly if they can live free."

"So would I," Will said. "So would I."

"Sleep now. We talk more later," Big Eagle said.

Will laid back down and closed his eyes. He was suddenly tired again.

Chapter Seven

The war-chief, with his second in command, Kiano, beside him, looked down from atop the white limestone pass at the blue column of soldiers slowly making its way along the winding road below. His eyes swept the terrain like those of an eagle, noting every aspect of the canyon-furrowed scene. The road ran through the timber, across the Sierra Diablo mountains and connected with several military outposts on the other side of Blackwell's Pass.

The soldiers were part of Colonel Gregg's brigade, on a mission to find and destroy Big Eagle and all of the remaining Quahadi Comanches. The army had kept the Comanches on the run for many months now, and the heaviness was taking a toll.

Kneeling and looking through his field glasses, Big Eagle saw two Kiowa trackers, uniformed in blue, serving as scouts. They rode point a half-mile ahead of the main body of the army. Side by side, in pairs, the army commenced in a steady, even trot. Half of the force rode in front of a water cart and the other half behind a six-mule wagon that carried a Gatling gun and some wooden crates. Beyond his view, the land south of him rolled away, dry and desolate.

In Comanche tongue, the two warriors communicated.

"Fourth Cavalry insignia," Big Eagle said to Kiano. He passed him the field glasses.

Kiano studied the troop and counted nearly one-hundred. "Once they are in the pass, Takala will close off their escape."

"Position six rifles up here," Big Eagle told him, motioning with his hand. "You and I will take them from the ground after they come out. This is as far as they go; we cannot allow them to come any closer to our stronghold. Make sure nothing happens to that gun wagon."

Bright sunlight glared off the rock-walls. Kiano, painted-faced and wearing a leather band tight against his head, squinted at Big Eagle and shaded his eyes with his hand. "The Kiowa scouts die first," he said, lowering his voice to a low whisper. "I only wish I could make those traitors suffer before I kill them. Maybe I will skin one alive."

"No prisoners," Big Eagle said. "Everything in blue dies here. Give the orders."

The two stood up, and moved noiselessly like a shadow, stepping down from the rocky hillock and over to the waiting horsemen. All fifty in the war party were armed with carbines, pistols and bows. They were bare-chested, with painted faces, and wore knee-high moccasins. Kiano explained the plan and split the group. The second half, led by pock-marked Takala, started down the steep slope to take up positions in what would become the rear of the two Fourth Cavalry companies.

Big Eagle and Kiano led their men down to the near end of the narrow pass where the road came out. A dozen of them dismounted silently and took positions in the brush, their figures blending into the earth, behind boulders and in shallow rills. The other nine erased all their tracks and took the horses into a ravine.

The two Kiowa scouts were the first of the cavalry to emerge. They trotted out in single file, checking their mounts and drawing rein fifty feet in front of the hidden Comanches. The lead rider raised the field glasses from around his neck, turning from one side to the other scanning the open plain and the pine forest beyond. He dismounted and walked forward a few yards, squatted on his haunches and examined the ground, looking for any disturbance of the soil.

"No tracks," he said, in Kiowa tongue. "Big Eagle is not near. If he was, we would have seen his sign."

"His sign," the second scout retorted, "would be our dead bodies. He would have picked us off already. But he has got to be hiding somewhere. We will find him."

"He is probably back in Mexico," the scout on the ground said. "Since jumping the reservation he spends more time in Chihuahua than in the Comancheria."

"Let him stay in Chihuahua," the other said. "Our posts and patrols will sleep better. I still cannot understand how two-hundred Comanches not only evade but constantly defeat eight-thousand soldiers hunting them."

"Bad army leadership. And smart Comanches."

"The army has got men covering every water hole between Big Spring and the Apache Mountains. They cannot—"

Thwack! The lead Kiowa scout stopped speaking mid-sentence, flinging up both hands, his face grimacing in agony. A feathered arrow jutted out of his belly, and bright red blood spurted from the wound. As the scout collapsed to his knees, with amazing speed Big Eagle raced out of the brush, knife in hand, and slashed the Kiowa's throat. He was followed by Kiano, who sprinted to the second horseman and dragged him from the saddle. As the Kiowa scout drew his pistol, the quickness of the Comanche overcame him, and Kiano gashed him with a steel-bladed tomahawk, once in the face and once in the skull. The scout groaned, then fell silent.

Four warriors rushed up. They dragged the bodies of the dead Kiowa scouts over and dropped them down the embankment, grabbed the horses' reins and led them to the ravine, then repositioned themselves on the lip of the rill. Big Eagle and Kiano, unslinging their carbines, waited in ambush beside the jagged outcrop at the mouth of the pass, watching and listening with the eyes and ears of a deer.

At the first sound and sight of horses inside the defile, Kiano ran back and passed word to the warriors in the ravine. He returned to Big Eagle, crouching low behind the rocks. They saw the horsemen come on and out from around the bend, passing in two's.

When a quarter of the troop was through and into the open, Big Eagle raised his Henry rifle, rested the long barrel on the flat surface of the rock, sighted on the back of the officer heading the column, and fired. The .44 carbine exploded; the lieutenant slumped in the saddle and tumbled from his horse.

A deadly volley of rifle and pistol shots rang out from the brush and the rocks; arrows flew in thick bunches, striking men and horses, and emptying saddles. Amid defiant battle yells of the Comanche, the blue column came apart in a welter of bloody, reeling confusion. Most of the troopers who managed to ride off were pursued by Comanche horsemen thundering up from the ravine and were shot before they had gone a mile.

At the same time, a shower of gunfire poured from the top of the slope and from the entrance to the pass. The air was thick with the crashing fire of rifles, the shouts of the Indian war whoops, and the cries and groans of the soldiers. Little groups of soldiers sought to make a stand here and there, but were soon swept away by the Comanche warriors.

When every bluecoat that had come through was motionless on the ground, Big Eagle leaped atop his pinto and, with Kiano and two others on horses behind, galloped into the defile. Through smoke and dust, he saw the water wagon, its driver dead, turned sideways, blocking the way. The wounded horse lay tangled in its harness. The Comanches quickly dismounted and pushed and pulled both animal and wagon far enough aside so that their horses could squeeze through. Remounting, they rode forward.

Then they neared the gun-wagon. Five troopers knelt on the ground beneath it, using its wheels and sides for cover and firing revolvers at Comanches twenty yards down the path. Big

Eagle and Kiano shot all five from behind and yelled to Takala to cease firing. They waited, heard no further gunfire, then saw Takala come running forward. His face was red with fervor and exertion, dripping with sweat and breathing hard, a pistol in his hand.

"We killed every soldier except seven or eight, who escaped on their horses," he told Big Eagle in Comanche tongue. Two fresh scalps hung from his pistol belt. "We were able to spare the mules. But we should get out of here fast. There is no telling where the rest of the brigade is. The ones who got away will warn them now."

Big Eagle put a hand on his shoulder. "Well done, Takala. This gun is a needed gift."

He slid lightly off his horse and jumped up onto the back of the wagon to inspect the Gatling gun. It was mounted on a bipod and chained to the wagon's slatted sides. With his knife Big Eagle pried open one of the wooden cases. It held new rifles. Stenciled on the lid was WINCHESTER '76 CENTERFIRE. There were several more, as well as crates of boxed ammunition. Kiano also jumped up to look, but only Big Eagle could read the English letters.

"I have seen one of these before. These rifles fire with great speed," he said. "They will be of much use to our fighters. Takala, come here."

He hurried over and stood beside the wagon. "Yes, Big Eagle."

"Take your men and head for the border. Cool your horses; water and feed them before you go. Make certain you leave tracks for the soldiers to follow."

"You *want* them to follow us?" asked Takala.

"I want them far away from the stronghold. Kiano's people will drive the wagons back, making sure to cover our tracks. Come back to camp in five days."

"Yes, Big Eagle," Takala said and went off.

Big Eagle turned to Kiano. "How many have we lost?"

"None. Two are wounded slightly. That is all."

"Good. Now we head for camp."

Before splitting up, the Comanches gathered all the rifles, pistols, shot pouches and powder horns from the dead troopers and loaded them into the wagons. They departed with Kiano and Big Eagle each driving one. Riders fanned out behind and in front of them. The entire war party headed west.

The Comanche camp, William Hart quickly noted, was full of hospitable women. Several had already been into his tipi, bringing fresh clothing and moccasins and serving him food and drink every few hours. The dark-haired woman who had tended him was now back with a clay platter piled with fire-roasted buffalo meat, and a colorful basket woven by split-willow that was filled with wild persimmons and nuts, which she placed before him on the earthen floor.

"Thank you, again," he said, sitting and smiling up at her.

She bowed her head a little and cast her eyes downward. Then she turned to go.

"Wait." He stood, a little shakily. "I want to talk to you. My name is Will. What's yours?"

She looked at him and he saw she did not understand English. "Thank...you," he said. He pointed to the food platter and to the clothes he was wearing and bowed his head once. "Thank... you...for...everything." She reminded him of a beautiful Natchez Indian girl he had once seen riding along the banks of the Mississippi River.

She smiled and hurried out.

He followed her, stooping somewhat to get through the thick, hide door flap, outside for the first time. He paused for a moment, lingering in indecision. There were several dozen tipis spread across a flattened ellipse and grouped between clusters of pinyon trees. Will observed that the tipis were sheathed with dried buffalo hides that had been sewn together and that the coverings were wrapped tightly around cone-shaped wood frames and pinned together with wooden skewers. Some of the tipis were decorated with stripes and designs of many shapes.

The thin shadows of early dusk fell over the landscape. It was near sunset and he stood watching the light recede. A stream flowed past the far end of camp and he could see several children kneeling at its bank and wading into the ripples of the water. No men were about, only women and children. The women wore beautifully tanned deerskin dresses with flared skirts and fringes, yellow and red beads that flashed in the brilliant rays of the lingering sunlight, and low moccasins with buffalo-leather soles.

A couple of young girls, their faces swarthy and wide-eyed, looked up from their basket-weaving with shy curiosity. Will smiled at them and he could hear them giggle. Nearby, an elderly woman was on her knees, leaning over a slab of rock, rolling and mashing corn into meal using a long oval stone.

On the far edge of camp, in a small grove of shade trees beyond the tipis, a group of ten or more women had gathered. Will noticed that there seemed to be something of great importance going on. He decided to walk over to see what was happening.

Coming up, he noticed a mound of freshly dug earth and a rectangular pit, a grave. The body of an old man who had died lay next to it atop a blanket of red and ochre. He had snow-white hair and two long braids intertwined with a single black-tipped eagle feather; his face was dark and wrinkled from many years. His cheeks were painted red, his eyes sealed with clay, and he was dressed in ceremonial breechcloth and buckskins. Several strands of colored beads hung around his neck.

The women attending him all preserved a decorum of somberness. Some of the younger women were crying. Two of the older ones bent over the body, spoke soft words, lifted the old man's knees and folded them against his chest. They wrapped him in another blanket, which they tied tight with buffalo-hide rope, and then placed him inside the grave in this sitting position. With wooden shovels they began filling in the pit with soil and rocks.

Will was taken by the sacred nature of this ancient rite. He watched in silence for a moment, and then he turned away and walked back toward the tipi. He noticed the sky was darkening toward the northwest. A cool touch of wind fanned his face and he could smell the promise of rain. He went back inside the tipi and lay down.

After a while he heard the rhythmic beat of hooves, the whinny of horses and the creaking of wagon wheels. The sound of shuffling footsteps passed outside. Going out, he saw Big Eagle and some of his war party returning. They parked their wagons in a clearing beyond the stream, climbed down, and were greeted by a group of women and children. One boy, about ten-years-old, began following Big Eagle and tugging at his cavalry holster. The war-chief said something, took out his revolver, removed the shells, and handed the pistol to him. Excited, the boy ran off with it as other boys chased after him. Will thought of Billy.

The woman who had tended Will was with Big Eagle now. She had an arm wrapped around his waist and hugged him tightly. The Comanche with the painted cheeks, walking beside him, was also with a woman. His arm was about her shoulder. The four walked together toward the camp. The rest of the group followed behind.

Night was coming on. In the distance, Will saw the flare of lightning once or twice on the northern horizon, and heard the low moan of rolling thunder. Fires began to glow in the camp as Big Eagle and the woman approached the tipi. The painted Indian and the woman with him followed them in. "Come in," Big Eagle called to Will.

He went inside. The women lit a fire. Big Eagle sat cross-legged on the ground, his strong hands clasping his knees, near the bed of sweet-smelling cedar. The woman lifted the platter of food offering it to Big Eagle, who shook his head, and then to the other two who also refused. Will stood behind them, waiting.

"I want to talk alone with this man," Big Eagle said to Kiano, in Comanche tongue. "Arrange for the distribution of the weapons. Later, we will go over tomorrow's plan."

"Why do you waste time with a filthy *white man*?" Kiano said, the flames of hate burning in his eyes, his voice deep and unwelcoming. "We should have let him perish on the *Llano*. I do not understand you."

From the way the painted Comanche glowered, Will had the feeling they were talking about him. And none too gently.

"This one is no enemy," Big Eagle said, his face lean and strong. "He speaks the truth. He has already helped us without knowing it. He shot the son of Sam Granger and one of his hired killers. But go now. I am sure Peytal will not mind being alone with you." He winked at the woman of Kiano.

The pair left and Big Eagle motioned Will down next to him, to sit in a place of favor beside the war-chief.

"You are feeling better, I see," Big Eagle said, poking the fire into a brighter blaze.

"I am. Thank you again for what you've done. I tried thanking the young woman here but I don't think she understood. Would you do it for me?"

Big Eagle said something to the woman in their language. She looked over at Will, smiled and nodded.

"Is she related to you?" Will asked.

"My wife. Her name is *Ta'by-yetch*. In English it means 'Sunrise.'"

"The name fits her. She's beautiful."

Big Eagle nodded in agreement.

"Do you have children?" Will asked.

"No longer. But once, I had two sons."

"Can I ask what happened?"

"They both died on the reservation. Of the cholera. My father and mother too. My wife's parents too." He said it matter-of-factly, showing no emotion.

"My first wife and my mother both died during the war. From fever." Will glanced at the woman. He tried to imagine what he and Beth would have felt if they'd lost Billy. Such pain was unimaginable. "You lived on the reservation with them?"

"Yes. At Fort Cobb, in the Oklahoma Territory. We were forced to go there. By your government. The soldiers and Indian agents promised we would be cared for. They all lied." He turned and spoke to his wife, who brought the food platter to him. He ate some of the meat and then a handful of nuts, popping them in his mouth several at a time.

The woman whispered something to Big Eagle and he turned to Will. "Sunrise says you should eat."

"I will, thank you."

Big Eagle handed him the platter. Will studied the war-chief in the flickering firelight as he ate. He had on a leather vest made of horsehide with no shirt underneath and Will could see the sinewy muscles of his arms and shoulders. His dark eyes were set deep in the sockets and his nose was curved. A bone-handled knife dangled from his belt and he wore a U.S. Army holster that had a pair of crossed swords on its flap. There was a presence in the manner and bearing of this man that reminded Will of Noble Caulder. This Comanche was a strong man not to be taken lightly, by friends or enemies.

"When did you leave Fort Cobb?" Will asked.

"Two years ago. When it was clear that the treaty which had been made at Medicine Lodge Creek was dead. I took out those of my people who had the courage to come with me to fight. Look quickly while we still live: what you see in this stronghold are the last free Comanches on earth."

"How many fighters do you have?"

"Two-hundred."

"What happened with the treaty?"

Big Eagle shrugged and put his arm around Sunrise. "The same that happened to every treaty. The white man broke it."

"How?"

"In all ways. Reservation lands were made between the Arkansas and Canadian rivers that no white was allowed to enter according to the treaty. We were to be fed and clothed."

"And you were not?"

"The Comanches were given food and clothing, yes. Bad, stinking food, rotten with worms. And thin clothing that fell from our bodies in the lightest rain or wind. The very old and very young became sick. Many died. Whites came and stole horses. They slaughtered the buffalo, for skins and horns, but mostly for sport. To watch the creatures die, and leave them to rot. They brought liquor and diseases. They sold guns and murdered Indians for their scalps: the Mexican government pays fifty dollars for a man's, twenty-five dollars for a woman's, and ten dollars for a child's. All this went unpunished by the white government."

Will sat silently looking square at the Comanche. The flames of the fire cast light upon the war-chief's face, and he saw that it looked sad. Proud as it was, it bore the look that comes only from continued defeat, disappointment and grief.

"Many Comanches grew angry." Big Eagle continued. "Some left the reservation and began raiding. So soldiers burned our camps and slaughtered our horses, because they know we are fighters from horseback. They killed five-thousand horses in this past year alone. Soon our horses will all be gone, along with the buffalo. All that will be left is their bones, mixed in with ours. So I fight. The army hunts me and my people day and night. I will never return to the reservation. The Comanche is a fugitive in his own land."

Will had seen courage before, in his own war, but none greater than what existed here, now, in this tipi. He sighed and looked at the woman. "What about her?" he asked. He was thinking of Beth. "What does she say?"

"Nothing. She is my woman. She goes where I go. When I die, she will take another husband, another warrior. They will live as long as they can. Then they, too, will die. Now I have a question for you. Why are you fighting this man Sam Granger?"

"Because," Will said, "he murdered my friend and left me for dead. He took over my town and made himself chief against everyone's wishes. He flouts the laws and makes his own wicked ones. He hurts people I care for, who can't fight back because they don't know how. Because they love peace. He preys on their weakness."

"You do not love peace?" asked the Comanche.

"I did, for ten years. Before that I was someone else—and my life was not very peaceful. I don't like him, but that person had to be brought back."

Big Eagle whispered something to the woman. She rose and went out.

The two were silent for a while. Will sat watching the beautiful red and yellow leaping flames and listening to the crackle of the fire inside the ring of flat stones and the chirping of crickets outside in the sagebrush. He looked over at the eagle-feathered lances standing in one corner, and watched the blue spires of smoke rising and filtering out the vent at the top of the tipi.

Big Eagle said, "Did you fight in the big war between the blue uniforms and the gray?"

"Yes."

"On which side?"

"The gray."

"Some of our people fought beside you in that war."

"I know it. They were noble fighters."

"You also know, then, what it means to be conquered and killed."

"I know that too. I also know that you can't beat the blue army, Big Eagle. Just as I couldn't. They're much too strong. You'll die."

Big Eagle nodded. "I am a warrior. The life of a warrior belongs to his people. I will give mine gladly if it means they can live away from the reservation even one day longer. We were born not on a reservation but on the prairie. There were no fences and everything drew a free breath. I want to die there, not within walls."

"So would I want to," Will said.

The woman returned, carrying a pitcher and a pair of small clay bowls, which she filled and handed to the two men. She placed the pitcher on the ground beside Big Eagle and went back out. He drank and motioned for Will to do the same. He raised the bowl, sniffed it a moment, and then drank it dry. The taste reminded him of a light sweet cider, only bitter. Big Eagle refilled their bowls.

"Have you any allies in your fight?" Will asked. "Will the Kiowa or the Apache join you?"

"The Kiowa," Big Eagle said, with disdain. "The Kiowa are weaker than women. They made a shameful peace with the soldiers and surrendered to them. Now they are slaves, as they deserve. Besides the Comanche, the only fighters left are the Chiricahua Apaches. But Geronimo and Victorio are far away in Arizona and New Mexico and are being hunted themselves."

"I wish there was a way I could help you."

"Why? Why should you wish to help the Comanche?"

"You were wronged. The law the white man gave you by solemn treaty was violated by him. Because I was once responsible for upholding white laws. And because I hate Sam Granger, your enemy. Somebody once told me that the enemy of my enemy was my friend. I forget who that was." He grinned.

The Indian stared into his eyes. "What do you intend to do?"

"Ruin Sam Granger. Destroy all he has. Then bring him to justice."

Now it was Big Eagle's turn to grin. "The Comanche is a fierce fighter, who makes war from horseback."

"I also fought from horseback, in the war of blue and gray. For four years. I will do it again, now."

"You were younger then."

"Yes. But I am still strong. And smarter than before."

"A warrior on horseback needs three things."

"Water for himself and his mount, food for them both, and… ammunition."

Big Eagle nodded. "I will give you all three. If you can draw some of Granger's men away from me, it is good."

"Thank you. I will. If you can lend me a horse, I'll leave in the morning."

"Are you well enough?"

"Yes."

"Where will you go?"

"Home, to my family. It's been three days. They don't know what happened and must be very worried. Then I'll get my guns and make for the high sierra."

"Did you hear any of Granger's plans?" Big Eagle asked.

"No. But if I learn anything that affects you, I'll send word. If I learn of any army movements, I'll send word."

"Granger must believe you are dead."

"I plan to keep it that way. If he finds out I'm alive, he'll hunt me. So he's not going to find out. Until it's too late. I'll be the hunter."

Big Eagle stood, stretched his legs and walked to the tipi entrance. "I will leave you now so you can sleep. The things you need will be ready early. It is a long ride east to the Pecos and your farm, across much dryness."

"You know my place?"

"I have seen it. Small, with a barn and a windmill and a garden. And a corral with a big spotted gray horse in it. Your son has hair like corn. Your wife has dark hair, like mine."

"So that was you I saw. Scouting with a war party?"

"Yes."

"And you let us stay."

"Why not? You have not harmed the Comanche. You have stolen no land and built no forts. A few acres along the Pecos are not much. Even whites must live somewhere."

Will swallowed hard. "Stay, Big Eagle," he said. "This is your tipi and your wife's. I can sleep outside. You've done too much already."

"It is nothing," the Comanche said. "Sleep well." He lifted the flap and went out.

Will fell asleep to the sound of heavy raindrops pattering against the buffalo-hide dome. He slept soundly until the rosy light of a new day filtered through the tipi. Just after sunrise the hide cover of the tipi opened and Big Eagle walked in. He held a new Winchester '76 carbine in his hand. Will stood up and greeted him.

"Everything is ready," Big Eagle said. "A horse waits for you. It carries ammunition and pemmican—dried meat that we pound fine and mix with melted fat. A little will nourish a warrior for many days. And here is water," he said, touching an oilskin pouch made of buffalo hide. "But remember the watering holes I told you of—you will need them." He handed Will the Winchester. "Here is one of the rifles I took from the soldiers. Take it."

"Thank you." Will turned it over in his hands, feeling its weight and balance. "It's a fine weapon, a cavalryman's weapon."

A Winchester short rifle, the gun was a .45-75 breech-loader with a fifteen-round magazine and a shiny twenty-two-inch barrel. The gun was brand new. He felt and smelled the coat of oil over the barrel, the lever, the action, and the checkered stock.

They went out into the morning air. The night's rain had been like a gift to the land, its last remnants sparkling like diamonds in the tufts of grass that dotted the camp. Will saw the spirited pinto, cream-colored and fully laden, standing in front of the tipi. Some Comanche women were already astir, carrying buckets of water to and from the stream. He looked for Sunrise but did not see her.

"Can you ride without a saddle?" Big Eagle asked.

"Yes," Will said. "Though it's been years since I have." He remembered his father lifting him onto a bareback pony when he was five and leading him along the Natchez Trace.

He handed the Winchester to Big Eagle, swung up easily onto the horse, and took back the rifle. Then he leaned down and extended his arm. The hands of the two men met in a firm clasp of friendship. "Say goodbye to Sunrise for me. And thank her again for her kindness. As for you: I'll never forget you, my friend. Never. I hope someday to see you again. Goodbye."

"Good luck," Big Eagle said, and walked quickly away from the horse and the tipi.

Will started off. Beyond the tipis, near a stand of pinyon trees, he saw the morning sunlight shimmering on the stream. He splashed across it. Stopping on the far bank, he checked the horse and cast a long glance back at the Comanche camp. He saw Big Eagle standing rigid and proud, gazing in his direction. Will raised his right arm and waved to the war-chief. Then he tugged the reins, put his heels into the pinto's flanks, and turned toward the *Llano Estacado*. He was homeward bound.

Chapter Eight

The sun beamed down warm, then hot; and the hours passed. Throughout the day, William Hart and the Indian pony journeyed through the glaring sun and dust-laden desert back to the Pecos. The sunset streaked the west with colors of red and purple, twilight fell and darkness settled in like a blanket. The cool air of the night was a welcome relief to both man and mount.

Will arrived home just after dawn. He came in from the west, shading his eyes from the morning sun, which poured a golden light over his farm. Off in the distance a rooster crowed. He dismounted beside the barn. Dusty and stiff, Will stretched his legs and led the cream-colored pinto into the barn. A few chickens were bobbing around, pecking at pieces of straw. He saw the familiar tawny-haired dog lying in a corner on a pile of hay. Lobo stood up when he saw Will, shook, stretched his paws and trotted over with his tail wagging.

"Hello, old boy," Will said, bending down on one knee to pet Lobo's head and muzzle. "How you doing, fella?" The dog licked his hand, and Will felt grateful for a warm touch. "How come you're not in bed with Billy?"

The dog looked at him expectantly.

He led the pinto into a stall, set his Winchester against the slatted brace, removed the pinto's bridle and brought over some oats and corn from a wooden barrel. Then he went into the stall next to it, where his appaloosa, Bedford, stood. The horse shook its head and snuffled.

"Hey, my friend," Will said. "It's good to see you." He patted its snout and stroked its withers. The horse nuzzled his shoulder. "You and I have work to do. Come on, let's go outside." He put on Bedford's bridle and reins and led him out into the corral, closing the gate behind. The horse tossed its mane and cantered in the split-rail enclosure.

Will ducked back inside the barn and grabbed a spade from the tool rack. He then returned to Bedford's stall, where he started digging in the left front corner. He had dug down about three feet when the shovel clanged against metal. He scooped out more dirt at the sides of the hole, knelt, reached down with both hands and pulled up a large strongbox with a handle on top and metal latches in front. He brushed off the excess dirt, unlatched the box, opened the lid, and removed three oiled sheepskins.

Opening the first, he unrolled his gun belt with the long-barreled Walker .44 revolver. Shells the size of pegs filled the ammunition loops. Next he unwrapped the shoulder holster that held the Colt .45 Peacemaker; then he opened the third oilskin which held another Colt .45, three boxes of shells, and two rolled-up bandoliers, filled with .45-caliber cartridges.

He slid the Walker .44 out and checked the firing pin, opened the cylinder and cocked and lowered the hammer several times. Turning the revolver sideways, he saw the W.H. engraved above the trigger guard and remembered the day in Natchez when Abell & Faulk, the best gunsmiths in the state, had fitted the walnut grips for him and cut the monograms. Coupled with Big Eagle's Winchester and the equipment he would get from Lucas Madison, these guns and ammunition would be enough to complete the work he had in mind.

Slipping the Walker .44 back into the holster, he put the metal box back in the hole, refilled it, then picked up the guns, slung the belts over his shoulder, placed the cartridge boxes inside his saddlebags, and started for the house.

Will felt a nervous pang in his stomach. *Beth has to know*, he told himself as he walked. *So let her see it. A picture is worth a thousand words. I never thought I'd have to tell her and hoped she wouldn't find out. But this is what it's come to. I can't hide my past from her anymore.*

Halfway up the path, the front door of the farmhouse opened and Manolo Sanchez stepped out on the porch, dressed in work whites, sombrero hanging over his back. His black head nodded up and down and he smiled toothily.

"Welcome home, *hombre*," Manolo said smiling broadly, coming up briskly and grabbing Will's shoulders. "Man, but we were worried." He looked at the purple-yellow facial bruises and then at the guns. "Can you walk with all that hardware?"

"Yes, man." Will stood looking at him and grinned. *"Como esta?"*

"Muy bien," Manolo said. *"Ahora.* Now."

"Bueno. Where's Beth? And where's Billy?"

"Your son is with his grandfather, in town," Manolo said. "The *señora* is *en la casa*, with Pilar. She sent the boy away after what happened at Spanish Red's the other night. When you didn't return, she feared for him. But they're all right. Nothing has happened. I watch them all the time. Pilar too."

"Thank God," Will said. "How is Beth?"

Manolo scowled and shook his head. *"Muy malo.* But much better now. We saw you coming, through the window. *Señora* is crying and laughing at the same time. Get in, *hombre.* And send Pilar to me, will you?"

"I will. And thank you, Manolo. Thank you."

Manolo started toward the barn, then stopped and turned around. "It's good to see you alive, my friend. We heard what those *cabardes* did to Sheriff Caulder. And about what you did to them in exchange. *Olé!* I'm with you in all things. Tell me whatever you need."

"Gracias, amigo. Right now I need my wife."

As he went up the steps, the door opened and Pilar was there. She had tears in her eyes. She put her arms around Will and kissed him once on each cheek, then stepped back and studied him. She caressed his face with both hands.

"Hola, Pilar. Thank you for helping Beth, *querida.* Manolo asks that you to come to him." He looked over Pilar's shoulder. "Where is she?"

"In the kitchen," Pilar said. "Go to her." She glanced at the guns but said nothing, kissing him again on the cheek.

Beth was sitting at the table with her chin on her hands. She did not look up. Will set his weapons down in a chair. Coming up behind, he touched her shoulders, bent over and kissed her cheek. "Hello, Beth," he said. "I'm sorry; I know you've been worried sick. It's so good to see you, so good to be home."

She jerked away and shook off his hands. "Don't touch me," she said without looking at him.

"Why not? Manolo said everything was all right. I thought you might be glad to see me. What's wrong?"

She raised her head and Will could see her nose running. Her eyes were red and bloodshot, with black patches below them. Tear-tracks marked her cheeks.

Beth began to laugh sarcastically. "What's wrong? You want to know what's wrong? I'll tell you what's wrong. Noble, our friend, is murdered. But you don't tell me. Instead, you tell me lies in church and skulk off in the dark, planning vengeance and murder."

"Justice," he said. "And I didn't lie; I just didn't tell the whole truth."

"It's the same thing. And then, while you're lying, you say I should trust you. Then you go to a saloon and murder two men, and—"

"It wasn't murder."

"No? What do you call two men shot dead by you?"

"I was trying to arrest them, to bring them in to stand trial for killing Noble. They drew down on me."

She continued, her voice rising, "Then you disappear for days and I don't know if you're alive or dead, or hurt, or in jail, or with another woman, or where, or what, or anything. Your son keeps asking me why you don't come home. He's bursting with pride because you killed people. 'I knew Pa wasn't a-scared of those men,' he says over and over. 'I'm glad he shot 'em.' Is this what we raised? Like father, like son, I guess. Now you show up, bringing *guns* into my house, bold as brass. Maybe the same guns you murdered those men with." She stopped, took a deep breath and said, "So go ahead and tell me, Will. And try not to lie. Where have you been? Who are you really? And what's happening to us?"

He reached for her but she pushed him away.

"Beth, I love you," Will said. "More than anything in this world. I love Billy the same way. If you never believe anything again, believe that. I'll tell you where I was: Sam Granger held me prisoner, bound me, beat me, and then brought me out to the *Llano Estacado* to die. Some Comanche Indians found me, brought me back to their camp and nursed me back from near-death."

She looked up from the table skeptically and sniffled. "Is that where you got those clothes? How did you get away?"

"They let me go; I wasn't their prisoner, they just wanted to help me. They gave food and water, and a horse. Then I rode home." He had no intention of frightening her further by going into too much detail about his brush with Granger or his experiences on the *Llano*. He felt a twinge of conscience at not disclosing all, but it could not be helped.

"I see from your bruises and marks that you've been beaten terribly."

"It's nothing."

She looked up at him in alarm. "Are these men coming after you? Here, to our *house?*" Her eyes widened.

"No, no." He thought quickly. "Sam Granger doesn't know I'm alive. He left me for buzzard-bait, and now he thinks I'm dead."

Beth stood up and turned to face him. "What have you brought down on us, Will? Who are you? We've been together almost ten years. I thought I knew you, but in one night you've become a total stranger."

He looked down and said nothing.

"Where are you going to go? Where? Oh, dear heavens, our lives are falling apart. Will, I beg of you, please don't go." Her throat quivered, her shoulders shook and she began to sob.

He took her in his arms and held her tight. She did not resist. "I love you, sweetheart. I love you, I love you," he said, kissing her lips and cheeks and neck. "It'll be all right."

But he knew the time had come. He had to tell her everything. Otherwise he could not do what he needed to do. If he was lucky, she'd be here when he came back. If not, the memory of their time together and their love would have to carry him the rest of his life.

"I'm the same as I always was, Beth," he said. "Trouble is, there's two of me. The one you know and the one I hid, the one from before you knew me. I thought the one from before was gone, I really did. But when they killed Noble the way they did, everything changed. I had to act."

He told her about the day Noble had come for dinner and what he had wanted and why. He told her how Noble had saved his life, on more than one occasion. How he had fought in the war. How Noble was responsible for bringing him down to Texas. How they had been lawmen together. How, if it hadn't been for Noble, he would not have met her.

She wiped her nose with a napkin and looked up at him. She looked over at his guns and bullets in the chair and then back up at him.

"You professed Christian beliefs all this time," she said. "When we first met, you said you'd been a cowhand up in Abilene, that you hated guns and the violence of the frontier. That you came to Enterprise to work on a ranch and live in peace."

"That part is true," he said. "I did come here to work, at Noble's invitation after he left El Paso and became sheriff of Enterprise. I rode the range for John Slidell for six months when I first came here, before we got married. Remember that?"

"I remember."

"It was quiet here the way I needed and longed for, and I believed in the peace. Peace is a beautiful idea, and I never expected to pick up a gun again. But I did lie about punching steers in Abilene. I was afraid if I told you the truth about the war and El Paso—after what happened to your Ma and with your Pa being a preacher—that you'd run away from me."

"I would have."

He nodded. "I know. But I loved you so much. I needed you more than I ever needed anyone or anything. And I wanted to be good to you and to care for you. Now more than ever."

She shook her head and bit her lower lip. Then she sneered. "You needed me. So you lied about the most important things, for your own selfishness. You tricked me. To get what you wanted."

"Yes. To get what I wanted."

"What else have you been lying about?"

"Nothing else."

"How can I believe anything from now on," she said, stiffening. "How can I ever trust you again?"

"Beth, it's haunted me ever since. But tell me true: haven't I been a good husband and father? Honest, truthful with you?"

Again she shook her head. "That doesn't matter now."

"How can it not?"

"How could you lie to me all this time? How could you kill people? Snuff out their lives? How do you do that?"

"It was hard. It never was easy. But I had a responsibility to keep the peace."

She laughed. "Keeping the peace through killing."

"Yes. I've killed men. First, it was enemies in the war. Who were trying to kill me. And after that, brutal men on the border, bandits and rapists and murderers, and still it was never easy; not once. And I did change, for you, Beth. I tried to build a life for us here. The farm's not much, I know. We'll never be rich. I love our place, but it doesn't need to be this place; it could be anywhere. Because for me, home is wherever *you* are. We can be happy again, when this is finished. I know it."

Her brow furrowed. She glared at him and he read betrayal in her eyes. "Have you really changed, Will? I think not. Not after what you did in the saloon. Not after whatever it is you're leaving me to do now."

"Yes. I have changed. The problem is that the world hasn't. There's cruelty and viciousness in it that we can't always avoid, no matter how much we want to. It found us. It killed the only man I ever loved. He was my brother, my friend, and I left him in the lurch when he needed me most. What do you want me to do? Go jump in the Pecos and forget about it? I'm going to end Sam Granger's reign of terror once and for all."

"Suppose there's more after him? And more after that? When does it end?"

"We'll hope and pray there isn't more. But if there is, we deal with it. Together."

"I loved Noble too," Beth said. "But going on a killing spree won't bring him back. Now you're leaving Billy and me in the lurch."

Frustrated, he shook his head. "My intent isn't to go on a killing spree. My intent is to stop Sam Granger and bring him to justice." All he could think to add was, "You're a woman and can't understand."

"Oh, no? I didn't realize that truth and lies and life and death were questions of gender."

He turned without a word and went into their bedroom and began removing his buckskins. Going over to the dresser, he poured water from a pitcher into the porcelain basin. He washed and shaved by the early morning sunlight—thinking about Sam Granger, his family, his beliefs—pulling the razor across his stubbled jaw. The thin light from the window fell upon his face, and in the reflection of the mirror he noticed a few silver hairs at his temples and the lined creases around his eyes. He wasn't a young, careless boy anymore. He had commitments and responsibilities. Commitments as a father and a husband. But he also had commitments to himself.

He grabbed boots from the closet, a denim shirt and moleskin pants, along with a range jacket and a dark brown, wide-brimmed Stetson Renegade hat. When he was dressed, he made a single crease in the felt Stetson and went back into the kitchen, his spurs clinking along the wooden floors.

Will picked up his pistol belt, strapped the Walker .44 to his leg and pulled the shoulder holster with the Colt .45 Peacemaker over his head. He lifted the cartridge belts and crossed them over his chest. He placed the second Colt .45 in his jacket pocket. Then he put on the Stetson.

Beth watched him with distaste. "Tell me something, Will. And try to make it believable, will you? Why did you give up what you did before you met me? What made you change?"

He knew the truth would be worse than anything he had said yet to her. But there was nothing for it. "A little girl, named Maria Ortega. Six years old, with wide brown eyes and a smile that would make you melt. Dead on the boardwalk, her dress soaked with blood. Shot during a gunfight on the main street of El Paso, that I started. Maybe it was my bullet that killed her. I'll never know. There isn't a day that goes by that I don't think of her."

Beth hung her head in silence.

Will saw horror on her face. He went to her and held her shoulders. She did not look at him. "Before I go," he said, "I need your forgiveness."

"For what?" she said, bitterly, in what seemed like both command and appeal. "For killing people? For lying? For leaving Billy and me alone? For doing whatever it is you're planning now? You want my forgiveness? You won't get it. Not for anything."

"Maybe," he said, "I just need it for having been born."

He bent to kiss her and she turned away. She reached back and with all her strength swung her right arm up and slapped him across the face. The slap made a loud cracking sound and left a red hand print on his cheek.

"I love you, Beth," he said, gazing into her face, disparately trying to etch every detail of her features forever on his memory. He looked at her for a full minute, then opened the door and walked out.

He wanted her to follow him, to call to him, to reassure him that everything was going to be all right. But he did not look back. He did not see her crying in front of the window as she watched him go, or hear her whisper, "I love you, too."

Chapter Nine

The sun was climbing as William Hart crossed onto the west bank of the Pecos River and turned north. Moving into the high country, past Barstow and Mentone, he rode along on Bedford, holding the reins of his pack horse, a sorrel mare name Tumbleweed. She was laden with the supplies and equipment that Lucas Madison had helped him sneak out of his general store without any of the regulators in town noticing.

Heading for the northern sierra where the view would command the stagecoach road, the unfinished Texas & Pacific railroad line, the silver mines, and Sam Granger's cattle spread, Will felt as if he were back leading the way for General Nathan Bedford Forrest. Only here the dry, mountain country was far different than the humid wilderness of Mississippi and West Tennessee. Still, after ten years working and riding here, he knew every trail and off-path in the Trans-Pecos as well he knew the ruts in the Natchez Trace and the names of the swamps along the Yazoo and Mississippi Rivers.

Passing through giant fields of spiked and thorny *cholla* cactus, prickly pear, and thickets of thriving mesquite growing up out of the hard, baked clay, he saw scorpions crawling over sand burs as big as cantaloupes, heard coyotes howling from distant rises, and watched lizards darting over broken, crumbling

crags of twisted rock and blasted buttes. Will kept on, stopping
only to water and rest the horses.

Time passed slowly in the shimmering afternoon heat. The
vast silence and infinite spaces of the great plateaus and flat-
headed mesas of West Texas made him feel he was the only man
left alive on earth. After a while, a red mass began to come closer
and fill more and more of the northern horizon, like an island
lost in a desert sea, rising up into an azure blue sky. Skirting
an enormous *caldera*, Will steered Bedford through a stand of
withered cottonwoods and toward the switchback that led to the
top of the approaching mass: Red Bluff.

As they climbed the path between black rocky outcrops and
low-hanging abutments, the switchback became so narrow and
steep and clogged with stones that the animals would go no
further. Will was forced to dismount, put on their hackamores,
and lead them by hand. The gravel and shale rattled, loosening
and falling beneath his feet; causing him and his horses to slip
and stagger most of the way up the zigzag path toward the
summit.

After several grueling hours, they reached the top, one man
and two horses, leg muscles twitching, dripping sweat and
gasping for air. Will removed the hackamores, placed them back
in a saddle bag, and brushed the sweat from both animals. He
removed a canteen from the coil of the lasso that was tied to his
black saddle, and then watered the horses. The three rested in
the shade of a defile until the sun began to set and evening was
coming on. He needed Bedford to be rested and fresh for the
morning.

Remounting, he rode easily across the flat, rocky, wooded
tabletop of the bluff until he reached a line shack in the middle
of a thicket, with an old handwritten sign on the door that said
"Line Shack #12."

Will knew exactly where he was. He had come here for a
reason. South of Red Bluff Lake and overlooking the Navidad
River, this line shack had been built before the Civil War

to shelter cowboys and range riders from the weather and marauding Comanches. It was the perfect base from which to operate: remote, hidden, and with difficult access. There was only one way up or down. A single rifleman, firing down the switchback, could hold off an entire regiment for as long as his ammunition held out.

They used to call Nathan Bedford Forrest the Gray Ghost, Will was thinking. *He always said that he rode where he liked and struck where he wanted. Now, these many years later, I'm about to strike like a ghost again. I wonder what my old friend from Tactics class, George Custer, would say if he was alive now and could see what I'm doing. Probably curse me for a Johnny.*

He tied up at the rear of the shack and began unloading supplies and hauling them inside. The shack was dark and had a musty smell of dry, rotting timber. Sultry streaks of dusk showed through the weathered roof where the crude shingle-slats had split. The floor was of bare dirt and a mount of spreading deer antlers hung on the wall.

When Will was done unloading supplies, he lit two big tallow candles, setting one on the table and the other atop a rusty pot-bellied stove. He then went back out and removed the Winchester from the rifle scabbard on Bedford's saddle and took it inside. He went out again, grabbed his bedroll, loosened the appaloosa's cinch, took off the black saddle, carried it inside, and dropped it in the corner next to the rifle.

Next, he used pieces of dead mesquite to build a fire in the stove and then brought over a coffee pot and cast-iron skillet. He reached into a leather bag for a bundled cloth, removed some jerked beef, bacon and biscuits, and fried the bacon in the pan while the coffee brewed. When everything was ready, he sat down at the little table. He drank the coffee, black, from a tin mug and ate the bacon straight from the pan, sopping up the grease with one of Julianne Madison's biscuits.

Finished, he put everything away and took out a pair of field glasses. He hung them around his neck and went out, walking through groves of pinyon and cottonwood and clumps of dense chaparral to the southern edge of the rocky tabletop. He put up the field glasses and scanned the black-fringed hills, plateaus and paths below, swinging the field glasses one-hundred and eighty degrees from side to side, taking in everything from the top of the bluff to the eastern horizon.

The sun was going down and gashes of red and gold streaked the sky. Dim stars were beginning to show white, stretching across the vast expanse, and Will saw the opaque outline of a pale round moon through the fading daylight. Below, there was no movement. The dusty road, trails, tan desert, brown mountains, dusky mesas and gray jagged peaks of the surrounding sierra looked as if they belonged to another planet.

Five miles off, Will could see dark, dead ash inside the bowl of the collapsed volcano that formed the *caldera*. The only signs of life were the buzz of insects on the cliff and the yelp of coyotes calling to each other somewhere behind him. He turned and focused the field glasses west, toward Sam Granger's ranchland, picturing where and how he would make the interception tomorrow. Will calculated the Overland Stage was due through at 11:30 in the morning.

Will took out his pocket watch. The sun was directly overhead, and sunlight glinted off the gold casing. He stared at the faded photo of Beth and Billy inside its cover for several moments before returning it to his side pocket. It was 12:08. The stage was late.

Sitting astride Bedford two miles from Red Bluff, he waited on the roadside. A hot wind blew, carrying fine red sand that stung his face. He was carrying two revolvers, the Walker .44 on his right leg and the Colt .45 Peacemaker under his left arm.

Finally, Will saw a dust cloud billowing beyond the far bend of the road. The appaloosa tossed its head, pointed its ears up, stamped a front leg, and snorted. Wheels clacked and hooves thudded louder as the stagecoach rolled into view.

Two men rode the bench. The driver, Hank Meacham, worked out of the Enterprise office for the Overland Company. Will had known him for years. The second man was a stranger wearing a long tan duster and a wide-brimmed black hat. He was the shotgun rider. Though Will had never seen him before, he knew perfectly well who the stranger worked for.

When the stage was a hundred yards off, he spurred Bedford out into the middle of the road and waved both arms, motioning for it to stop. The driver slowed his six-horse team and brought the coach to a creaking halt. Meacham pushed down on the brake handle with his foot.

"Yo, there," he said, his whip lying across his lap. "What gives, mister?"

Saying nothing, Will nudged Bedford and took him around the coach, looking in the windows. There were no passengers. He brought the appaloosa to the left side of the bench, where the shotgun rider sat, and called up to the driver.

"Hank," he said. "I'm here for your cargo. Toss it down, please." He tilted back the brim of his Renegade so the driver could see his face.

"Will? Will Hart? What in the name of…?"

The regulator beside Hank Meacham grabbed for his shotgun but stopped in mid-reach. He stiffened, threw up his hands and splayed his fingers, staring at the long-barreled .44 leveled at him.

"You don't want to do this, brother, believe me," the regulator said to Will. He was bearded and thick-necked with bushy eyebrows and squinty eyes. "You don't know who this cargo belongs to. You don't want to find out."

"Actually, I do know," Will said. "That's why I'm here. Send it on down, Hank." His eyes were fixed on the regulator's hands.

"Will Hart," the driver said in a Texas drawl, with a half-smile. "I heard you was dead, killed the other night. I'm glad it ain't true. But you will be if you don't give this up. Have you gone plumb *loco*?"

Meacham was in his late fifties, paunchy, with a sun-burned face, chubby cheeks and a double chin. He had been an Overland Stage driver for as long as Will could recall. He remembered him as an affable, friendly man who loved to tell jokes and talk. There were times when the two of them had coffee and pie together over at Ma Hanley's.

"It's all right. Sam Granger doesn't need the blood money. And nobody in Texas will cry when his killers miss a payday."

"Ain't that the truth. Granger and his hired gunmen have the whole county scared to death."

"Throw it down, Hank," Will said. "Don't make me ask again."

Meacham reached into the boot and brought up a double-handled leather satchel with an accordion flap. He shook his head. "I hope you know what you're doing, young fella. I always liked you, Will." He heaved the grip down to the ground. "Granger will chop you up for stealing his payroll, you know that."

His eyes and gun on the regulator, Will slid off Bedford, picked up the satchel, opened its zipper and glanced inside. There were stacks of flat smooth bundles of brand new bills piled high and banded with red paper strips.

"This money just came from the Lone Star bank," Meacham said.

"Looks like it was just printed in the U.S. Treasury," Will told him. "How much is here?"

"Wait, I got a receipt," Meacham said, reaching into his shirt pocket and taking out a slip of paper. "I'll tell ya exactly." He unfolded it. "$20,575.00. it says."

Will whistled. "You boys make a pretty penny," he told the regulator. "But there'll be no women and champagne tonight."

"What're you aiming to do with the money?" the regulator queried. "Make a run for the border? The boss'll track you down in Mexico, or anywhere else. There's no place to hide. Before you spend six bits I'll find you myself."

"You won't have to."

"No? Why not?"

"Because the money's staying right here."

The regulator raised both eyebrows. "What do you mean, staying here? What are you going to do with it?"

"Burn it. Every last Yankee greenback. And you get to watch. I might even put out word that you stole it. See what your boss thinks about that."

With his left hand, Will reached into his pocket, took out a stick match and flicked his thumbnail over the head. As the match flared and Will looked in the bag at the money, the regulator made a quick swipe for his double-barrel shotgun, swung it into position and pulled back both hammers.

He was not quick enough. Before he could squeeze the triggers of the double-barrel, the Colt .45 Peacemaker jumped twice in Will's hand, flashing fire and belching smoke. Both slugs tore through the regulator's chest. The first lifted him from his seat; the second blew him off it.

The team of horses whinnied and jerked in the harness at the explosions. Bedford snorted and reared. Patting his haunch and tightening the reins to steady him, Will dismounted and walked over to the regulator. He was lying on his left side, hat on the ground, eyes closed, right arm extended over his head as if reaching for something. His trail coat was twisted about his knees. The shotgun lay on the ground beside him. Will kept the revolver raised, but saw there was no need for another shot. The first two had finished him.

Holstering the Colt, he went around to the satchel on the other side of the stagecoach. Squatting, he took out another match, struck it against his boot-heel, and reached down into the bag, carefully lighting the ends of three bill-stacks. Then he brought up the match and waved it out. The money caught fire and began sending up a stream of gray smoke.

"Tar-nation!" Hank Meacham said from the driver's seat. "Dang!" Bug-eyed, he stared down at the dead man. Then his eyes squinted and he looked at Will, crouched beside the burning satchel. "Aw, Will, you kilt him right next to me. I jest about felt the air singed by them slugs! A second ago I was talkin' to the fella. I can't believe what you've done."

Will said nothing. He stood and watched the smoke floating up from the bag.

"Listen, Will," Meacham said. "I ain't going to tell nobody it was you. I'll say we was held up by road agents in masks. Or else Granger's men got to come and hang you."

"Thanks, Hank. But it's all right. Go back to Enterprise and tell Granger the truth." He watched the bag burn a moment more, then reached for Bedford's pommel, stepped up into the stirrup and swung into saddle.

"The truth? You cracked? Look, nobody in Enterprise will side with Granger against you. You're already a hero for what you done at Red's place. We'll all help you if we can. Swear to anythin' you want."

"I appreciate it. But I want them to come after me."

Meacham frowned. "You want 'em to? How can you fight off an army?"

"I'm not about to get back-shot, cramped up and pinned down or ambushed in town, like Noble. Out here in the open I'll see them coming. I'll be a ghost. Ever try hunting a ghost, Hank?"

"Can't say I have."

"This ghost shoots back."

He nodded. "I already knowed *that*. What about him?" He tossed his head toward the body.

"What about him?"

"What should I do with him?"

"Take him back to town with you. That way you'll stay out of any trouble with Granger."

Meacham nodded and clambered down. Will dismounted. They lifted the body and placed it inside the coach. Then Meacham slammed the door and climbed back up onto the stagecoach. Will remounted Bedford and rode up close to the driver's seat.

"One more thing, Hank. I want you to deliver a message to Granger."

"Sure."

"Tell him Will Hart's canceling his railroad and silver profits for a while. The Salt Draw shaft is about to close, and no boxcars will be reaching his spread anytime soon. Granger will have to load farther up the line; drive his beef along the Chisholm through Comanche territory. If they let him. I don't think they will."

"Whaddya mean?"

"He'll know soon enough. If he'd like to discuss matters, I'll be waiting near Red Bluff. You hear? *Red Bluff.* And Hank—tell Granger and Devlin I'll be attending the funeral."

"What funeral?"

"Theirs," Will said. *"Adios."* He spurred the horse.

"I will," Meacham said after him. His face rippled with a smile, and he slapped his thigh. "You sure are one sure spit-fire. But I'll tell him everything. Good luck to you, Will!"

The next morning, as a pink dawn splashed the margin of the eastern sky, Will stood at the foot of the bridge. This was his favorite time of day. Cool and clear, calm and serene, the air was sweet-smelling as the sun dried up the moisture of the night. He stood between Bedford and Tumbleweed all set to go to work. The sticks of dynamite Lucas Madison gave him, along with other blasting supplies, were ready, taped into tight bundles like the ones he used to blast out tree stumps on the farm. Dynamiting would be the easy part; the last task of the day. Tonight, the prairie dogs and rattlers would have a front-row seat for the fireworks. *Tonight,* Will thought, *will be like the Fourth of July.*

Now was the tough part, the hard labor. Many years had passed since he'd torn up railroad track and blown up bridges. Then, the Confederate Army provided plenty of help. Alone, the destruction would take all day. He grinned as he remembered how Forrest's raiders were famous in the Yankee newspapers for wrecking fifty miles of track a day. Well, if he could get a half-mile torn, that would hurt Granger enough and stymie the work of the Texas & Pacific—especially here in the heart of the Comancheria. The railroad men would have to arm themselves and work slow, with no sleep, one eye always on the lookout for Comanches.

Comanches. Will wondered where they were. With safe passage from Big Eagle, Will could go where he wanted. Any other white man daring to come in here was taking his life and his scalp in his hands. Big Eagle despised railroad workers; not only did they bring in white land-grabbers, they shot buffalo off the backs of the railroad cars for sport.

Railroad wrecking is something Big Eagle would like, Will thought. *I wonder if he'll hear of it.* But it seemed nothing happened in these parts that the war-chief didn't hear about.

He looked down into the dark, rocky, hundred-foot-deep gorge. Taking a pair of rawhide work gloves, a heavy crowbar and a sledgehammer from the pack on Tumbleweed, Will hauled the tools over to the first transverse wood cross tie and began prying up and breaking the spikes that fastened them to the rails. Laid across the gravel at three-foot intervals, he figured to rip up at least five-hundred ties.

Tearing up track was as brutal as busting rock on a chain gang in Huntsville federal prison. Bare-chested and streaming sweat, he worked his way down the line through the clear sunny morning and deep into the heat of the afternoon, pulling and prying and banging and lifting and hoisting and tipping. He took water breaks in the shade underneath the bridge, where he tied the horses and removed their loads; it was a huge relief to be out of the hot sun, even for a minute.

He noticed a few rattlesnakes slithering in and out of rock-crevices and watched hawks soaring high and swooping down on the snakes. He hummed favorite old Southern spirituals while he labored, wet with sweat. He thought of places and people—of Beth and Billy, Noble and Preacher Cullen, John Slidell, Tishomingo Creek, Forrest, Natchez, Sarah Hart, El Paso, West Point, Sam Granger, Zach Marlowe, Ike Devlin, the *Llano Estacado*, Big Eagle, Spanish Red's and the Longhorn saloon—where the sarsaparilla was cold—until his mind grew numb from exhaustion and all he could think of were these infernal railroad sleepers that stretched on and on into the distance and into infinity.

By six o'clock, he was a half-mile out from the bridge. The sun was beginning to ease and slanting westward. After a break, he trudged back to the horses. He fed and watered them, put on his shirt, took out some food and sat eating under the bridge. He wolfed down two biscuits and some jerked beef, then washed it down with warm water from his canteen. He grabbed a few jugs of kerosene from Tumbleweed's pack and went down the line, shaking out the smelly liquid, dousing the cross ties and striking matches on his way back, setting the wood on fire.

In short order, the ties were all burning. Oily black smoke rose and spread across the high plateau. It would take the Texas & Pacific railroad quite some time to restore this section of track, because there would be no bridge on which the railroad cars could stop and unload new sleepers and hardware—time during which Sam Granger could ship no beef or bring in supplies for his mines. Time during which he would lose plenty. Supplies would have to come in on mule trains, his cattle driven out by drovers.

The bridge was today's next order of business. Just before dark, with eight bundles of dynamite in a burlap sack, he moved gingerly down the slope and climbed out onto the crotch of a heavy wooden brace. Working his way down, using his hands and feet and stepping carefully, he stopped about twenty feet from the floor of the gorge. Looking up, he saw the high, dark underbelly of the bridge, with some whippoorwill nests built in the upper braces. He removed a section of rope from his bag and lashed his first bundle to a support beam.

He clambered sideways, fifty feet across toward the opposite end of the span, parallel to the spot where he'd tied his first bundle. He wedged in another, lashed it, and climbed higher, repeating the process until all the bundles were placed.

Finished, he crawled and shimmied his way along the struts toward the horses. Jumping off a beam and onto solid ground, he saddled Bedford and reloaded the supplies on Tumbleweed. Mounting the appaloosa and leading the sorrel, he rode a quarter-mile from the bridge, up a brown hillock and into a clump of scrub brush. He tied both animals tightly to a tree, put on their hackamores, and removed his field glasses from around Bedford's pommel. He slid his Winchester from the saddle scabbard and walked back to the bridge, cradling the carbine in the bend of his left arm.

Dusk was settling as Will scrabbled down the rocky slope. He found a small outcrop, sat down on it and looked for his dynamite. He spotted the bundles in his field glasses, noticing several sticks sweating tiny beads of nitroglycerine. These were unstable and it was good to be rid of them. He lowered the field glasses, took bolls of cotton from his shirt pocket and stuffed them in his ears. He picked up his rifle. Raising the front sight, he levered a round, tucked the butt into his shoulder, pressed his right cheek against the stock, aimed, and fired.

The shot cracked loud in his ears and reverberated under the bridge; the bullet missed, chipping off a chunk of wood several inches from the dynamite bundle. Will adjusted the sight-blade, chambered another round, and raised the Winchester. He fired again. This time, he found his target. There was a cracking boom and a blazing light, like a bolt of lightning. Will fired again at the next bundle, and the next, and then the next. Each round found its target with a thunderous explosion; clouds of fire-filled, reeking smoke billowed up into the sky.

Eardrums throbbing, nostrils twitching and lungs burning, Will jumped up, back-pedaled thirty yards, sank to his knees and raised the field glasses. There was exhilaration to demolition, and he confessed a keen enjoyment and an elemental thrill that ran deep and made him shiver. As he watched, the top-center of the span appeared to rise several feet in the air before lowering inches at a time. Then, all at once, it settled and fell in on itself, like an avalanche. The bridge collapsed in the center as if hit by the artillery of a thirty-two pound Parrott. Pieces of wood and strips of iron track cascaded into the gorge like a waterfall.

When the avalanche subsided and the smoke began to clear, Will eased toward the edge of the slope and looked down with his field glasses. The floor of the gorge was littered with broken lumber and shards of metal. Stumpy, jagged, saw-toothed slabs of brace were all that remained of the thick buttresses.

Night, soothing and still, was coming on. Only a low moan of wind in the pinyons broke the sudden stillness. Weary but satisfied, Will went to the horses.

"Well, team," he said to them, patting their muzzles. He mounted Bedford and started off toward Salt Draw and the foot of the Apache Mountains. "One more piece of business and then we'll get some shut-eye. We're going to dynamite one of old Granger's mine shafts."

Sam Granger sat on the front edge of the desk in his study and stared red-faced at the two men standing before him. The top button of his shirt was open and his tie hung loose around the collar. It was late afternoon and Ike Devlin had just brought the news.

"You told me Hart was dead," Granger said. "You lied. I don't like being lied to."

"I didn't lie, Mr. Granger," Devlin said, turning slightly pale. "He was as good as dead when we left him."

"He's alive now, isn't he? And McAllister's corpse is on the Overland Stage."

"Hart didn't have more than a few hours left, I swear. If it was up to me I'd of plugged him that night in Red's. Only we wanted him to suffer. So we made him suffer and left him to rot in the *Llano*, just as you ordered." He turned to the man beside him. "Tell him, Surtee."

"It's true, Mr. Granger," the other said. "I was there, I seen it. It's just like Ike says. That fella was beat up bad, nearly gone. I can't figure how he kept alive, let alone got out of that desert."

Angry, Sam Granger's voice grew lower and flatter. "Well, he managed to survive somehow. He's already killed my boy and my top gun. Now he's cost me a fortune, a mountain of ore, and weeks of time. The lost time is as bad as the lost money. Twenty grand, up in smoke! I promised the War Department I'd extend the rail line through the Pecos by next month. It's political suicide if I can't meet my own commitment. Hart's sitting out there laughing and taunting me, planning who-knows-what else. I can't allow any more delays. I want him dead. *Comprende?"*

"Yes, sir," Ike Devlin said. "What do you want me to do?"

"What do you think I want you to do?"

"Form a posse and light out after him?"

"We know where he is," Granger said, tight-jawed, gritting his teeth. "So go get him. Don't come back until it's done. Or maybe I'll send somebody to find *you.*"

Ike Devlin shook his head. "It's got to be a trick. I mean, why would he tell us where he is?"

Granger was becoming more impatient and annoyed by the second. "So what if it's a trick? He's one man. Arrogant, dangerous, but still only one man. Take as many guns as you need. You're supposed to be professionals. I shouldn't have to tell you how to run a man down. Hound Hart. Corner him. Get him."

"Oh, we'll get him," Ike Devlin said. "Don't worry. We'll get him."

Will spotted them early, from the top of the bluff. Squatting and looking in the field glasses, he saw their dust cloud. The dark group of horsemen and mounts pulled into view, fifteen miles out. There was still plenty of time.

They came on in single file, strung out along the road in the mid-morning sun, the ten of them reminding him of a Yankee patrol. He thought of Noble and remembered their old outfit ambushing Union cavalry at Corinth and Memphis and a hundred other places across three states.

Instead of wearing blue, this bunch wore long trail coats covered in dust. Will took the field glasses and moved the sites slowly across the faces of the horsemen. He wondered if any of these regulators had fought for the Union, and if so, in what units. *They might've survived the war,* he said to himself, *but their luck's about to run out.*

Fully armed, cartridge belts crossed over his chest and carrying three revolvers, he stood up and led both his horses, their eyes covered, down the switchback to the foot of Red Bluff. The riders were still some miles off. He removed the hackamores and lifted his canteen from Bedford's saddle, unscrewed the cap and took a long drink. He lowered the canteen, took a deep breath, raised it again and swigged some more water, this time rolling it around in his mouth, then spit it out on the sand. He put his foot in the stirrup on the appaloosa's left side and swung into the saddle.

Putting up the field glasses again, his eyes roved the terrain and watched Granger's posse of regulators come on. When they were a mile off, Will reached back into his saddle bag and took out one stick of dynamite. He pulled a match from his shirt pocket, struck it against his shoulder holster and lit the fuse. He flung the stick out in front of him—it sailed forty feet—and waited.

Bang! the explosion kicked up a geyser of prairie dirt, spraying rocks in a dozen directions. Bedford and Tumbleweed reared and circled. Will yanked hard on their reins, pulling them tight and short and letting the animals spin under control, slowing and sidling them until they stood still.

The regulators stopped short; their mounts sputtered and reared. Then they spotted the single rider, sitting motionless at the base of Red Bluff. Will saw the lead horseman, Ike Devlin, look through a pair of field glasses. Will looked back in his. He lowered the field glasses, slid the Winchester carbine from the rifle sheath, slung it over his left shoulder, took off his Stetson and waved it at Devlin. Putting his hat back on and pulling it down, he took the big horse out from under the shadow of the bluff and began to ride.

He spurred Bedford into a trot, turned him east, and began tapping his heels in, quick and firm and steady. He bent forward now over the saddle horn, riding low and light, both hands loose on the reins, toeing the stirrups, his backside two inches up off the leather, the wind rushing past and turning up the brim of his Stetson. The appaloosa began to gather steam and run faster and faster, opening up until he was flying full bore across the plain. Tumbleweed, even without pack, saddle, or rider, ran a full length behind, straining to match Bedford's great stride.

"C'mon, Bedford, run, boy," Will said. He stroked and patted the appaloosa's neck. "That's it, run! Nobody can catch you."

The horse's smoke-colored mane streamed backward as he sprinted; the wind whistled in their ears. Will continued talking and patting and they galloped on, down into a ravine. Will felt Bedford's muscles heaving between his thighs as they crossed the gully bottom and started up the far bank. Kicking out dirt with his back hooves, Bedford surged upward. He was climbing the steep slope. He was across the ravine.

The regulators followed hard but were falling behind. Will unslung his Winchester, levered a round and fired a shot over his shoulder. He could not hit anything at this distance—they were a good mile and a half back—but he wanted them angry and motivated to continue the chase. He knew he had time and that their horses were no match for his.

Finally he reached the rock-rimmed horseshoe that was Red Bluff Canyon. He slowed Bedford to a trot and took him inside. The sorrel trotted up next to them. They stopped. Will looked up. Colossal walls of mountain-faced cliff rose several hundred feet, with small, white, flat step-rocks like stairs cut into its sides glistening in the sun. The ground within the tremendous bowl was grassy and full of withered clumps of trees, stumps and boulders, sinking into deceiving depths. Thickets of tall pinyon trees stood like sentinels on either side of the entrance. *There's only one way in and out of a box canyon,* Will thought. *Let's see what you can do, Devlin.*

He slapped Tumbleweed hard on the rump and hollered "Yaaah, go!" to make him run deeper into the canyon. The horse ran forward twenty yards and stopped. Will drew the Colt .45 from his shoulder holster, yelled "Go!" again, and fired once in the air. The sorrel resumed running. Turning Bedford now, he sped back out of the horseshoe, veered off into the pinyons on his right, leaped down, tied the horse, unslung his carbine, ran up behind a tall boulder in between two trees, and waited for the regulators to arrive.

They did. Checking their mounts, coming on slow and wary as they approached the entrance, they stopped, glanced around and listened. Leaning against the shady side of the boulder, feeling its coolness, Will gripped his carbine with both hands. He heard the quick breathing of tired horses and then the men talking. Bunched in a tight circle, Ike Devlin had his back to Will. The regulators were no more than twenty yards distant.

"If we ride in there after him," Devlin said, "he starts picking us off from someplace."

"Hart ain't as good as the boss thinks," the man next to him said. It was Terry Surtee, whose dark hair hung to his shoulders beneath his hat. "There's no way out of there. 'Less he climbs the canyon walls. 'Less he's part goat. Even if he tried, we'd see him, shoot him off."

"He can't take a horse up them walls," another regulator said. "I say wait here. Thirst him out. He's got to run dry sometime."

Ike Devlin raised his field glasses, twisted around in the saddle and peered into the canyon.

"See anything, Ike?" Surtee said.

"I see a sorrel all the way back of the bowl. Grazing, looks like."

"No rider?"

"Nope."

"No other horse?"

"Nope."

"What you make of it?"

Devlin lowered the field glasses. "I make him hiding out someplace in there. Hoping to draw us in. The only thing these Reb cowards know is how to hide."

From behind his rock, Will laughed to himself, half amused, half irritated. *Yankee idiots*, he thought. *You blue bellies should never have won the war. You're too darn dim-witted.*

"So what do we do?" Terry Surtee said. "We won't get a more perfect chance to catch him. We can't go back to Mr. Granger without Hart's body."

"And we won't," Ike Devlin said. "It ends here. All we got to do is wait. We'll make camp over past the foot of the cliff. C'mon." He stepped down from his horse and began to lead it away from the canyon mouth. Several of the others dismounted and followed him.

Just then, from out of the pinyons Bedford began to snort shrilly and whinny when a yellow-jacket stung his nose.

Devlin stopped short and turned on his heel. Crouching, he yelled, "Hart's here! Take cover!" He pulled out his pistol and began firing in the direction of the neighing.

The others all drew their revolvers and commenced shooting into the trees, the roar of gunfire echoing off the canyon walls.

Spinning to the edge of the boulder, Will began pumping lead from his Winchester. Bullet after bullet tore through the shocked mass of regulators and horses; the carbine crackled from behind the rock. The regulators fired in the direction of the boulder; bullets barked the pinyons and chattered off the top of the slab. Crowded together and caught out in the open, five men and two horses fell screaming in short order.

Panicked and throwing wild shots, the other five backed away, ducking and weaving. They scrambled and chased after their spooked horses, bending low trying to escape the fusillade. As they snatched rein, toed the stirrups and turned tail, Will stepped out into the open. Ike Devlin, whipping his horse on both flanks, thundered off ahead of the others. Will levered his carbine and aimed for him, fired, missed, fired again, and missed again. He swung the Winchester and nailed three riders that were close, blowing them from their mounts before they made a further fifty yards. One other rider, his long hair streaming in the wind, was escaping behind Devlin. Will wanted them both; he wanted them all.

Running into the pinyons, he checked Bedford, saw he was unhurt, swung up into the saddle and took out hard after the two regulators. Racing after them, he fired and fired, emptying his carbine.

He drew his Walker .44 and fired three shots at the nearest man, the long-haired one. The third bullet found him. The rider's arm jerked limply, flinging his pistol. His body sagged and he pitched forward in the saddle, falling out sideways, losing his hat. He rolled twice, tried to get up and began crawling toward his horse. The animal ran on a few yards ahead of him and stopped.

Pulling up beside him, Will slid down from Bedford. He went over with the Walker .44 cocked and pointed it at the man's head.

Terry Surtee saw him and fell onto his back as if in surrender. Breathing heavily, his eyes were glazed and watering. Will knelt, picked up his pistol and tossed it away. A bullet had ripped through the top of Surtee's right arm. Will holstered the Walker, rolled up Surtee's shirtsleeve, tore off a long strip of cloth and bound it tight around his forearm.

"I remember you from the *Llano*," Will said, kneeling. "You're one of the ones who took my boots while Devlin tied a rope around me. You laughed then. You thought it was funny. Think so now?"

"I…I didn't mean it. Are…are you going to…kill me?"

"This is your lucky day, *pistolero*. I'm not going to kill you today. But if I ever see your face again, I will. Today, I need you to deliver a message."

"I…I don't know if I can ride."

"If you want to live," Will said to him, "you've got to ride. You might lose the arm, but at least you'll be alive."

Surtee stared up at him and nodded.

"I owe Devlin for the *Llano*. Tell him I always pay my debts. And tell Sam Granger that he hasn't seen anything yet. Tell him that after I'm finished with his operation, I'm coming for him." He went over to Surtee's horse and led it back, then lifted the wounded man and helped him into the saddle. "Can you remember what I just told you? Say it back."

Hunched forward and clutching the pommel with both hands, Surtee repeated the message.

"Good. What's your name, boy?"

"Terry Surtee. Thanks for not killing me, Mr. Hart."

"Well, Terry. You'd better ride fast. Make sure you tell Granger exactly what happened here and what I said. Now, go!" He whacked the horse's rump and watched it gallop off.

Mounting Bedford, Will went back toward the pinyons. He put up his field glasses and scanned the area. There was nothing in sight, only turkey-buzzards circling overhead. The remaining regulators were all dead. Two horses were badly wounded. He shot them both from the saddle, then rode into the canyon to retrieve Tumbleweed.

When he came out, on foot with the sorrel in tow and the Winchester in hand, he stopped when he saw an approaching rider. It was Terry Surtee.

Will leveled the rifle at the returning regulator.

"Don't shoot," Surtee yelled. "I've got something I need to tell you."

"Come ahead, slowly," Will said. The regulator drew rein and pulled up six paces from Will.

"What is it? Did you forget my message for Granger?"

"No, I wanted to warn you."

"Warn me about what?" Will queried.

"Uh, I heard Granger and Devlin talking about a trump card they said they'd use if they needed."

"What trump card?" Will asked. "What do you mean?"

"Your family."

Suddenly Will was filled with terror. *What if Sam Granger did decide to go after Beth and Billy—to get back at him?* Will had witnessed first-hand how cruel Granger could be, so how could he have under-estimated his heartlessness? He knew Granger would stop at nothing to get what he wants. *But this was unthinkable.*

"What else do you know about this?" Will said, trying to keep his voice from trembling.

"That's all, Mr. Hart. Believe me."

"Thank you, Terry. Now go."

Will swallowed hard. His heart felt like it was going to beat out of his chest. The rest of his plans would have to wait. He quickly watered both horses, and mounted Bedford. Tugging hard at the reins, he put both heels into the flanks, and headed south toward the Pecos.

Though he did not know it, Will was not alone. Two men had been watching him all morning and witnessed the action from high atop Red Bluff Canyon. Just now, as he rode away, one stood looking through a pair of field glasses. The other knelt beside him on one knee. Both were shirtless in the afternoon heat, both carried carbines slung over their shoulders and bandoliers of ammunition crisscrossed over their chests and wore knee-length moccasins. The one kneeling, with the painted face, was Kiano. The other man, standing and watching Will through the field glasses, was the Comanche war-chief, Big Eagle.

Chapter Ten

Something was very wrong. There was an eerie silence over the family farm this evening that William Hart had never known. Approaching his home from the west, he took out his pocket watch: it was 6:30. The corral was empty, the gate open. Why? And where was Manolo? Everything seemed still, breathless. There was not a bird singing in the trees or a single jackrabbit scampering through the sagebrush. Even the barn was quiet. A woman's shuddering wail, like the mournful cry of a coyote, pierced the silence. He was gripped by a sickening coldness in his chest. He spurred Bedford.

Coming toward the house, he stopped beside a reddish bundle. The dog, Lobo, lay motionless on his side. His eyes were closed. Blood stained his fur below where a bullet had entered. Further up, at the bottom of the porch steps, was Pilar. She sat on the ground, cradling Manolo in her arms. She kept rocking him, back and forth, like an infant. Tears rolled down her cheeks and dripped onto his face. Lying on his back, Manolo had a bullet hole in his left side. The front of his white shirt was soaked with blood. He was unconscious, but alive and breathing.

Will jumped from the horse and ran up the walk. He fell to his knees beside Pilar and put his arms around her. He felt sick. He did not have to ask what happened; he knew: Sam Granger had left his calling card.

Pilar raised her head and stared into his eyes. Lips quivering, her voice broke as she spoke. "They come and take them...your wife and son," she stammered. Her shoulders shook. "Manolo, he try to stop them and...they...shot him. Look what they do, Will. My Manolo, *mi pobrecito*," she stuttered. She began to shriek again.

"*Querida,*" Will said. He held her tight. "Shh, I know, I know. I'm so sorry. He is still breathing. We can help him. There is still time. But I need all your strength now to talk to me. Which one did this? How long ago? What happened to Beth and Billy?"

Pilar took a deep breath and quieted. "*Quien sabes?* Ten, fifteen minutes, maybe. They come for you," she said, sobbing a little, "six *pistoleros* in long coats. When you are not here, they are angry. They say you damage their business and kill many of them. They say you will only stop if they take your wife and son. When they put their hands on the *señora*, Manolo—" she began crying hard again, "—try to take a gun and...the *rojo,* he shoot him in front of us. The *señora* and I are screaming and the boy is crying and trying to fight them. Then the dog tried to protect us, and the *rojo* shot him. He say if you want your family back, you must ride to the Granger *rancheria* and give yourself up. Only then can they be freed."

Listening to Pilar, Will carefully washed and dressed the wound, then bandaged it tight. "This *rojo malo*, did he have a name?"

"I hear them say *Devlin.* But it should be the devil: *el diablo!*"

"Did he hurt you, *querida?*"

"No." She was sobbing again.

"Did he hurt Beth?"

"No. But the boy..."

"What? Tell me."

"He hit him when he try to protect the *señora*, but he's not hurt bad."

Good boy, Will thought.

"Pilar, I'm going to hitch up the buckboard and lay Manolo in the back on a bed of hay and blankets. I want you to ride into Enterprise and go to Doc Bransom's office; if he's not there, go to his home. Can you do that?"

"I don't know if I can. *Mi esposo, mi amante.*" She leaned over Manolo, holding him tighter.

"You've got to. Manolo needs a doctor. We both have work to do. Right now, these *pistoleros* have to pay for what they've done."

"Ah, Will!" she wept. "What if he dies? How will I live without him?"

"He won't die. But we need to get him help *pronto.*" Gently, Will rubbed the face of his *Segundo.* "I love him too."

When the buckboard was ready, Will drew Pilar's arms away from her husband, lifted Manolo and carried him to the buckboard. Pilar followed. Will helped her up onto the seat and handed her the reins.

"When Manolo wakes up, tell him I'm sorry," he told her. "And tell him that the whole family will be there soon to see him."

"You will go to the *rancheria?*"

"I will, but not in the way they think."

She leaned over and wrapped her arms around him. "Return with them, Will. *Por favor.*"

"I will, *querida,*" he said, stroking her hair and kissing her cheek. "I swear I will."

The Granger compound was dark and still. By the dim light of stars and moon, Will's eye roved the property. The ranch house itself stood along the rough corner of the largest of the three narrow canyon walls. Corrals and barns and sheds lay in the foreground. No light shone in the pair of bunkhouses or in any other out-buildings. In the main house, one second-floor window glowed with a flickering yellow light.

Positioned on a wooded rise a hundred yards out, Will lay on his stomach studying the place through his field glasses. He wondered if Beth and Billy were being held in that second-floor room. He had not seen much of the house the night Devlin brought him there and could only guess at the layout.

The full moon was sinking. Sunrise was no more than an hour off. Will noted some open windows on the lower floor offering a point of entry. He saw several slow-pacing regulators patrolling along the barbed wire that surrounded the compound. Getting past them would be easy; finding his family, quietly, would be the tricky part. Though well-armed, he did not want to shoot his way out of the *hacienda*, not with a woman and boy alongside and several dozen regulators likely on the premises. He remembered little Maria Ortega on the boardwalk in El Paso. Subterfuge would be the better part of valor here.

He stood and went over to Bedford. He lifted the Winchester from its saddle sheath and tied the horse firmly to the thick branch of a cottonwood. He then eased out of the woods, into the berry brush and mesquite that dotted the ranchland facing the compound, dropped to his stomach and crawled toward the barbed wire fence. Fifty yards in, he stopped, listened and raised the field glasses. The regulators were far away and far apart. He covered the remaining distance and lay flat for a moment, unmoving in front of the wire, recovering his breath.

He raised himself on his elbows. He peered through the field glasses again and scanned the house. It was a rich man's house, with no adobe, all polished stone and stucco. It had huge glossy oak double-doors, like the doors of a cathedral. A veranda, with wicker furniture on it and covered by a light-colored awning, stretched across the right side of the *hacienda*.

Will took a pair of cutters from his back pocket. He squeezed tight, snipping the wire. He ducked through, crouched, and looked for signs of movement. The dark figure of a lone sentry stood fifteen yards away and Will could make out the dull-red end of a cigarette and smell the smoke.

Will lay flat, stretching his long length beside a clump of withered sagebrush, and waited patiently. He slipped from his position and glided noiselessly on his elbows, being careful not to break twigs nor rattle stones. He stopped less than ten feet from the regulator, near an orchard of pecan trees.

Will waited, silent as a shadow. When the time was right, he slowly rose to his knee, took a deep breath and with a swift bound lunged at the regulator, clasping his right hand over the man's mouth and wrestling him to the ground. He wrapped his left arm around the regulator's neck and closed tight and hard, until the man lay prone and motionless. Will removed the regulator's long trail coat.

Will stood, slipped on the trail coat, pulled the Stetson low over his forehead and walked past a line of sheds and corrals and a bunkhouse. Nearing the main house, he looked around, vaulted a fence and darted close to the *hacienda*. Mounting the wooden stairs, he stepped onto the long porch. He looked up at the sky. The stars were still shining in the vast blackness. There was about half an hour of dark left, just enough time.

Going to an open window, he slid it up further, bent down, put his right leg over the sill and then his left. Unmoving, he listened and heard nothing but the ticking of an unseen clock. In the black darkness, he struck a match. It sizzled and flared; he was in a grand room with a high ceiling and discerned the outlines of sofas, overstuffed chairs and tables. A big stone fireplace was lined with ash, and the room smelled of it. Off the room's end was a foyer leading to a staircase, toward which Will went. He climbed the steps lightly, holding the banister, and stopped when one creaked. He listened, heard nothing and continued on to the top.

There, he peered down a long carpeted hallway. He noticed half a dozen closed doors and one that stood ajar. Light streamed out into the corridor from the room. He kept to the shadows of the walls and continued. After taking three steps, he felt the hard barrel of a revolver press into his back.

"Stop, right there," a female voice hissed.

Will turned and saw a familiar face in the shadows. It was Magdalena, the young woman who had let them in the *hacienda* the night Ike Devlin had hauled him here from Spanish Red's. He recalled the day she accompanied Sam Granger to Noble's office. Now she wore riding pants and a denim shirt. Her dark hair fell over her shoulders.

"Ma'am," he whispered. "I'm here for my wife and son."

Startled, Magdalena studied his face. Then she recognized him. "I almost shot you. I thought you were one of the *pistoleros*, that you wanted to hurt the woman and the boy. We must get them out. Men will be coming. Follow me." She put her finger to her lips.

She took his hand and led him down the hallway and into the lighted room. It was empty, with a four-poster bed and a roll-top desk in it. She lifted the hurricane lamp from a bureau, walked out and motioned to him. They went to the last room on the right. With Will behind her, Magdalena opened the door.

Will saw Beth and Billy sitting huddled together on a sofa along the back wall. The boy had his arm around his mother's shoulder. Billy looked up.

"Pa!" Billy said in a loud whisper. "Ma, Pa's here!"

Beth raised her head. She had been crying, and her eyes were swollen and red. She reached out for Will expectantly, her hand trembling. His eyes fixed on hers and his heart leaped; they were all right. Even in this grim moment, Beth's beauty and sweetness—immense and everlasting—clutched at his heart.

Just then, from the corner of his left eye, he saw a black blur of movement. He grasped for his Walker .44, but it was too late. Ike Devlin stepped out of the darkness and fired. The bullet clipped the top of his left arm, burning through the shoulder and coming out his upper back. He felt scalding heat and sharp pain. He wheeled, fell to his knees and crumpled to the floor on his side.

"Will!" Beth called out. "Oh, Will, Will!" She looked at Devlin. "What kind of monster are you?" She began to cry.

"Well, now," Ike Devlin said, turning the revolver toward Magdalena. She held the lamp in one hand, her gun in the other, and wore a shocked expression. He grinned. "Didn't expect to find me here, huh? Aren't you the little traitor? Helping the enemy now, eh?"

Devlin took Magdalena's gun, and kicked Will onto his back. He reached inside Will's coat, checked him for weapons and removed all three of his pistols. He tossed everything onto a chair and whistled. "That's what I call *armed*," he said.

"Pa!" Billy shouted. Will stirred and tried to stand. "Ma, Pa's okay!"

Keeping the gun on him, Devlin went over to Beth, yanked her hair and jerked her head sideways. "You married one dumb farmer man. He walked right into the trap. All you can do now is die along with him."

"Leave my mother alone!" Billy said and slapped at his hand.

Will got up slowly, and braced himself against the frame of the door. "Stay calm," Will told them, the trail coat crimson with blood, his left arm hanging useless at his side. "And we'll get out of here." He had no idea how he would pull that off, but it sounded right. He said to Devlin from somewhere, "You're a dead man, Ike. I'm going to plant you."

Devlin took two strides toward him and cracked him in the temple with the pistol butt, dropping Will to one knee. Beth gasped.

"Not so dangerous now, are you, without your guns. It's you who's dead, farmer."

At that moment, Sam Granger came barging in, grizzled, a revolver in one hand, and a kerosene lamp in the other. He set the lamp down atop a table and looked strangely at Magdalena. He went to her, took her lamp and set it down.

"What are you doing in here, dressed like that?" he asked.

She looked at him without answering. Ike Devlin said, "Helping Hart, Mr. Granger. She brought him here, showed him where they were. To spring them. Had a gun for him and everything."

"Is that true?" Sam Granger asked, his eyes firing.

She looked at him with defiant loathing. "Yes," Magdalena said. "Every word. *Es verdad.*"

"Why would you help my enemy, go against me?"

She laughed bitterly. "You kidnap an innocent woman and child to murder them, and ask me that? I heard you planning it with this *asesino*—this killer. I've heard too many things for too long. *Bastante!* I've had enough of your evil."

Sam Granger's lip curled below his mustache and began to twitch. He lifted his right hand and hit Magdalena across the face. His gold ring cut her and left an imprint. "Ungrateful tramp," he roared with rage. "After all I've done for you."

She held her hand to her cheek and laughed again. "Done for me? You mean murdering my husband and buying me, like a slave, from my father because we were poor and had no food? Each time you touched me my skin crawled. Pig," she said. *"Puerco."* She spat at his feet and he slapped her twice.

"I gave you the opportunity to be a great lady of society, instead of a *peón* eating with the dogs. Now, it's too late. Get rid of all of them. And I mean all of them," he told Devlin. "Away from here. Make sure the bodies aren't found. Then maybe we can finally get back to work and accomplish something."

Sam Granger started out, stopped and came up close to Will. He studied him a moment and said, "You're a tough *hombre*, Hart. Maybe the toughest I've ever known. You've caused me a world of grief and cost me a lot of time and a ton of money. You killed my boy, so now I'm going to kill yours, along with his parents. I hope Roy was worth their lives to you. Because that's the exchange. That's the price you pay." He turned and left.

"All right," Devlin said, prodding Will with his pistol. "You," he said, looking at Beth. "Up. Everybody move into the hall and down the stairs. We're taking a little trip."

The darkness of night had paled and the gray of early morning met them as they went out the big heavy doors and onto the porch. Walking beside Magdalena and holding Billy's hand, Beth leaned close to Will and sobbed, "What are we to do? You and I are one thing, but our son?"

Will was as frightened as he had ever been. *Hold on to yourself,* he said in his head. *Otherwise you're no good to them.* He prayed, *Lord, if ever there was a time for a miracle, let it be now. Not for me, but for Beth and Billy—they're your innocent children, they've done nothing wrong.*

"It's going to be all right, Beth," he reassured. "We—" Suddenly, off in the distance, Will heard the low trampling of horse hooves and the crack of gun fire. He stopped and listened. The sound of the hooves grew louder and another shot followed. There was no mistaking it: the report of a carbine. Three more shots, one after the other.

Four regulators came racing out of the cottonwoods in tandem and riding across the sagebrush toward the guardhouse where the fence opened on the south side of the *hacienda*, riding low, their long coats flapping, spurring their horses and whipping their reins side to side in a frenzy.

Another shot rang out, louder now, closer, and the horseman nearest the trees fell out of the saddle. The regulator manning the guardhouse burst from the wooden shack and flung open the gate as the three remaining riders came flying in and screamed at the top of their lungs, "Comanches, right behind! The hills are crawling!" The guard ran inside his guardhouse.

Will saw two long-haired, shirtless Comanches, their chests and faces painted, sweep up out of the trees. Shooting Winchester '76 rapid-fire carbines, they galloped to the gate, leaped down, opened it, broke into the shack and shot the guard. They ran out and threw the gate wide open, remounted and resumed firing at the men inside the corral. Bullets flew; three regulators fell, along with their horses. The regulators in the corral tried to draw rifles from the scabbards but their horses were rearing and beginning to panic under the hail of bullets. The men started to run, firing their pistols and scurrying for cover. The air was full with puffs of bitter smoke.

Hearing the gunfire, half-dressed, half-shaved men ran out of the bunkhouses with pistols in hand and were shot down as they emerged. Will saw clearly who the two Comanche shooters were—Big Eagle and Kiano.

"Go back into the house!" Will screamed to Beth, ripping off his trail coat and hurling it to the ground. "Go, Billy, stay with Ma and take cover! I'll be back. Go, Magdalena, go!"

A large group of warriors, four dozen at least, came thundering out of the trees and rode to Big Eagle. They joined in the shooting, laying down blanket fire and raking men, horses, and buildings all across the compound. Still more warriors poured from the cottonwoods, and Will realized that Big Eagle had brought his entire band, all bent on revenge and the complete destruction of Granger and the buffalo-killers. The war-chief waited for the last of his riders to come up, then the entire company poured through the open gate like a flood.

Ike Devlin spun his mount. He cocked his revolver and aimed a parting shot at Will. As he fired, Will, five feet away, jumped down from porch, sprinted toward him, reached up with his good hand and tried to drag him down. The horse reared, thrusting Will aside, and the regulator rode off.

"Big Eagle, Big Eagle!" Will yelled, running to a riderless mare and swinging up.

He spurred it left, riding low and fast to avoid the bullets and catch up with the war-chief, still calling his name. Big Eagle was now past the corral and headed toward the bunkhouses and stables. Will needed to reach him before the warriors mistook him for a Granger man.

Somehow in the noise and confusion, Big Eagle heard the sound of his name being shouted in English. He reined in his pinto, turned, saw Will, recognized him and galloped over.

"We decided to join you in the battle," Big Eagle said. "I hope you do not mind."

"They took my family. I came for them. You saved us. Give me a gun. I'm going to find them."

Big Eagle drew the .44 Army Colt revolver from the cavalry holster at his side and handed it to Will. "Take something else." Reaching into a pocket, he removed a small clay container. He dipped his finger in, reached across and painted blue marks on Will's cheeks and forehead. "My men will not harm anyone wearing my mark."

Will slipped the gun into the holster on his leg. "We'll meet when this is over," he said. "And Big Eagle—my wife and son and another woman are somewhere back in the main house. If you see them, don't let them be hurt."

"No one will touch them," he said. He yelled to Kiano in Comanche tongue, then said to Will, "We have work here."

Will nodded and rode off toward the main house.

Devlin's horse was back at the *hacienda*, standing tied to the hitching rail in front of the veranda. Will dismounted, drew the Army Colt and started up the steps. At that moment the heavy oak doors opened and the regulator came out, holding Beth. Billy was nowhere in sight. She was squirming and trying to get away. Shocked at seeing Will there with a gun, Devlin spun Beth in front of him like a shield. He hooked one arm around her neck, drew his pistol and pointed it at her head. He dragged her down the steps past Will and over to his horse.

"You move, I take her skull off," he said.

"Will!" Beth gasped.

"Easy, Ike," Will said. "I'm not moving, see? But you can't get out of here. It's over for you as well as Granger. Let my wife go. Then I'll let you go." He watched Devlin's hands. "I can't speak for the Comanches, though. They're angry with you boys for some reason."

"Will!" Beth gasped again.

"Easy, honey, it's going to be okay," Will said. "Where's Billy?"

"Inside, with Granger," Beth said, struggling to free herself from Devlin's grasp. "He's keeping him, stuffing money in a bag."

"I'm going to get on my horse," Devlin said. "Now, lose that gun or she dies. You twitch wrong, she dies. Now, toss it way over there."

"All right," Will said and tossed it.

Still pointing the gun at Beth, Devlin eased his hand away from her neck to step up into the stirrup. At that moment, she thrust her elbow at him to knock the pistol away. As his arm went up, Will rushed him and Devlin pulled the trigger. Beth screamed as the shot flew high and ricocheted off the *hacienda's* stone facade.

Then Will was into him, ramming a shoulder to his chest and driving him to the ground. He smelled Devlin's sour sweat as they fought, rolling, grappling beneath the underside of the skittering horse. The tethered horse snorted and stamped. The regulator brought up his pistol. His left arm crippled, Will grabbed Devlin's wrist with his right hand and shook it, trying to jar the gun loose.

Neither succeeded. Grunting, his whole body straining, Devlin, on top, tried kneeing him to break his grip. His kick missed; Will shifted on his back and took the blow on his hip. Hands still locked on the pistol, both men struggled, panting, knowing this was to the death. With one hand, Devlin clutched at Will's throat. At that moment, Will freed the pistol and with one single motion, thumbed the hammer and fired. Devlin swiped out at Will's gun-hand, but not in time to stop the explosion.

Devlin jolted back, wheezed, dribbled saliva and stiffened. In his face was a forbidding darkness, suspended in some dusky purgatory between life and death. He tried to get up, but his strength waned and he fell onto his face. The horse above them snuffled and stutter-stepped away.

Will got up slowly, feeling dizzy and weak in the legs. Beth ran to him and threw herself into his arms. "Oh Will, are you all right?" she said in horror.

"Billy," Will said. "I have to...get him." He collapsed to his knees.

Just then a dozen Comanche horsemen rode up and stopped in front of the *hacienda*. Kiano and Big Eagle were in the lead. The war-chief slid off his pinto and walked over to them. Beth shrank back against Will, cowering.

"It's all right, honey," Will said. "He's my friend."

Beth stared at him without understanding. Bleeding from his wound, his face painted like an Indian's, she was shocked and deeply frightened.

Big Eagle glanced at the body of Ike Devlin. He bent down and fingered Will's shoulder on both sides, making him wince. "A clean wound," Big Eagle said. "I can bind it."

"My son's inside, with Sam Granger," Will said, struggling to stand. "The young woman too. I have to get them."

"*I* will get them," Big Eagle told him. "It's time I looked upon this butcher. Wait here."

"My son!" Beth said, weeping. "What if he hurts him?"

"Trust this man," Will said to her. "I owe him my life. I trust him with Billy's. If he can't save him no one can."

Big Eagle looked at Beth with no expression. He nodded to Kiano and Takala and the others. He spoke a few words in Comanche tongue and they came off their horses, carbines in hand, and went up into the house.

Will felt Beth's light touch on his right arm, moving downward, and felt her small, trembling hand slip into his. He grasped it and they stood, huddled together, holding hands and waiting.

Long minutes passed during which they listened to the gunfire sounding across the compound. Finally a single pistol shot rang out from the house. There was a pause and then a woman's scream. This was followed by a long, agonized, guttural cry of a man, more animal-sounding than human. A single rifle shot; then silence.

Moments later the double-doors groaned open and Magdalena ran out. She hurried over to Beth. Then came Big Eagle. He was carrying Billy under his right arm, holding him parallel to the ground. Next was Kiano. There was blood streaked along both his silver wrist bracelets and spattered across his chest. In one hand he held his steel-bladed tomahawk; in the other he grasped the wet scalp of Sam Granger. Takala came next, flanked by two warriors who were helping him to walk. He had a gunshot wound in his upper thigh. The rest of the Comanches remained inside.

Big Eagle set Billy on his feet beside his mother. The boy continued staring in awe at the war-chief. Laughing through her tears, Beth tried hugging him. But Billy wriggled away and spun around to his father.

"A Comanche warrior, Pa!" he said. "I never thought I'd see one. This is better than Christmas! Isn't he something?"

Will looked up at Big Eagle's rugged handsomeness and smiled. "That he is," he told his son, arm around his shoulder. "He sure is something."

"You too, Pa," Billy said with a big hug.

Big Eagle walked back up the steps of the *hacienda*, opened the doors and yelled in. Leaving them open, he went over to the leather bag on his horse and removed one of the clay-and-meal poultices he carried. Coming to Will, he took his arm from his shirt and dressed the bullet wound, wrapping the moist cloth tight around his shoulder and below his arm.

By the time he was done, the rest of the warriors had come out of the house and were mounting their horses. Will looked up and saw smoke in the windows of the upper floors. On the lower floors, in the big room, flames were beginning to rise. "What now?" he said to Big Eagle.

"Nothing of this *rancheria* will remain. We will burn it all. Not one long-coat will be left alive. It is being done now." Will could still hear gunfire but it was much more sporadic and less intense than before. Sam Granger and his regulators were finished.

His arm around Beth, Will said to Big Eagle, "I'm embarrassed to ask you another favor. But my appaloosa is tied, about a hundred yards out there in the brush"—he pointed—"and I haven't the strength to—"

Big Eagle went to his pinto, swung up lightly and said something to one of his men. The man rode off and returned quickly, leading Bedford by his reins.

"Go home," Big Eagle called down to Will. "Here are two more horses. Go back to your farm. Your fight is over." He looked at Beth and then at Billy. "Raise your son together."

Will thought of Big Eagle's lost children.

The boy squinted up, drinking in everything there was to see about the war-chief.

"What is your name?" Big Eagle asked him.

"Billy."

"Billy, your father is a skillful warrior and a brave man, as mine was. Honor him. Your mother, too."

Will left Billy and Beth standing beside Magdalena and walked up beside Big Eagle's horse. "I have no words to thank you. I owe you more than I can ever repay. You have saved my family and you have brought peace again to Pecos County. You are a true peacemaker, Big Eagle."

Big Eagle smiled, his eyes radiant in the morning sun. "You were the one who reminded me that peace is a treasure worth seeking."

"You are always welcome on our farm, anytime and for any reason. I want to see you again."

Big Eagle shook his head. "My days as chief of the Quahadi Comanche are numbered. I have received word that Victorio was hunted down and killed in Arizona and that Geronimo is ready to surrender. But I will keep fighting the soldiers. I will never surrender."

Will nodded. "I know."

Will went to Kiano, sitting on his horse beside Big Eagle, and reached up to him. "Thank you," he said.

Kiano sat unmoving, glaring down at him. Then a faint crease of a smile came to the Comanche's face and he reached down and took his hand.

Will went back to Big Eagle. He reached up and the two clasped hands. Then Big Eagle turned his horse, called to his men in the Comanche language, and rode off at their head.

Billy stood watching the warriors ride away. When they were out of sight, he turned to his father.

"Pa," Billy said, holding out his hand toward Will's gun belt. "Can I see your pistol? Can I hold it? Please? Can I?"

Will looked at Beth. She did not say anything and made no gesture either of affirmation or denial.

Will slid the .44 out from the holster. His own guns, the ones with his initials carved into them, were upstairs in the *hacienda* and would be destroyed in the fire. He felt glad, as though a burden was being lifted. He opened the cylinder, ejected the shells and spent cartridges and handed the gun to his son.

"Holy mackerel," Billy said, wide-eyed and grinning. "It's heavy!"

"Four pounds," Will said.

"Tommy Miller told me he heard you used to be a marshal. Is it true?"

"It's true."

"Were you a fast draw?"

"No," Will said.

"Why not?" He sounded disappointed.

"Speed from the holster isn't important; that's only in newspapers and dime novels. What matters in a fight is which man comes with more force. Which has more strength in his mind and soul."

"All right, that's enough of that talk," Beth said, annoyed. "I don't ever want to see a gun again."

"Me either," Will said, hoping it was true. He took the gun back from his son and slipped it back into the holster.

Thick black smoke rose from the compound and they could hear faint cries coming down on the wind.

"Can we go now?" Beth said, looking around. "It's still dangerous around here."

"Take the pinto there, Billy. Magdalena can ride the sorrel. Your mother and I will ride Bedford."

"Can I have him? As my very own?" Billy said, eyebrows raised.

"Yes, consider him a gift from Big Eagle."

"Wow, what should I name him?"

"I don't know, Billy. What do you think you should name him?"

"Noble," the boy said proudly. "I'll name him Noble."

"I think that's a fine name, son."

Mounting Bedford, Will helped Beth slip up into the saddle behind him. She wrapped her arms around him tight and pressed the side of her face against his back.

"Let's go home," Will said, tugging the reins and heading south.

Dawn faded and the eastern horizon peaked with a pageant of pink and yellow, turning brighter as the morning sun rose over a ridge.

The sunrise over the Pecos never looked more beautiful.